WITHIN
THE
SPELL

WITHIN THE SPELL

JacQueline Vaughn Roe

ISBN: 978-1-950536-92-4

Joy,
I wish you were still coloring
at the table across from me as I write.
I miss you, but I'm glad you're free.

To my favorite son, Caleb:
May you be as loyal as Paul
As strong as Jacob,
And as joyfully hilarious as Amis.

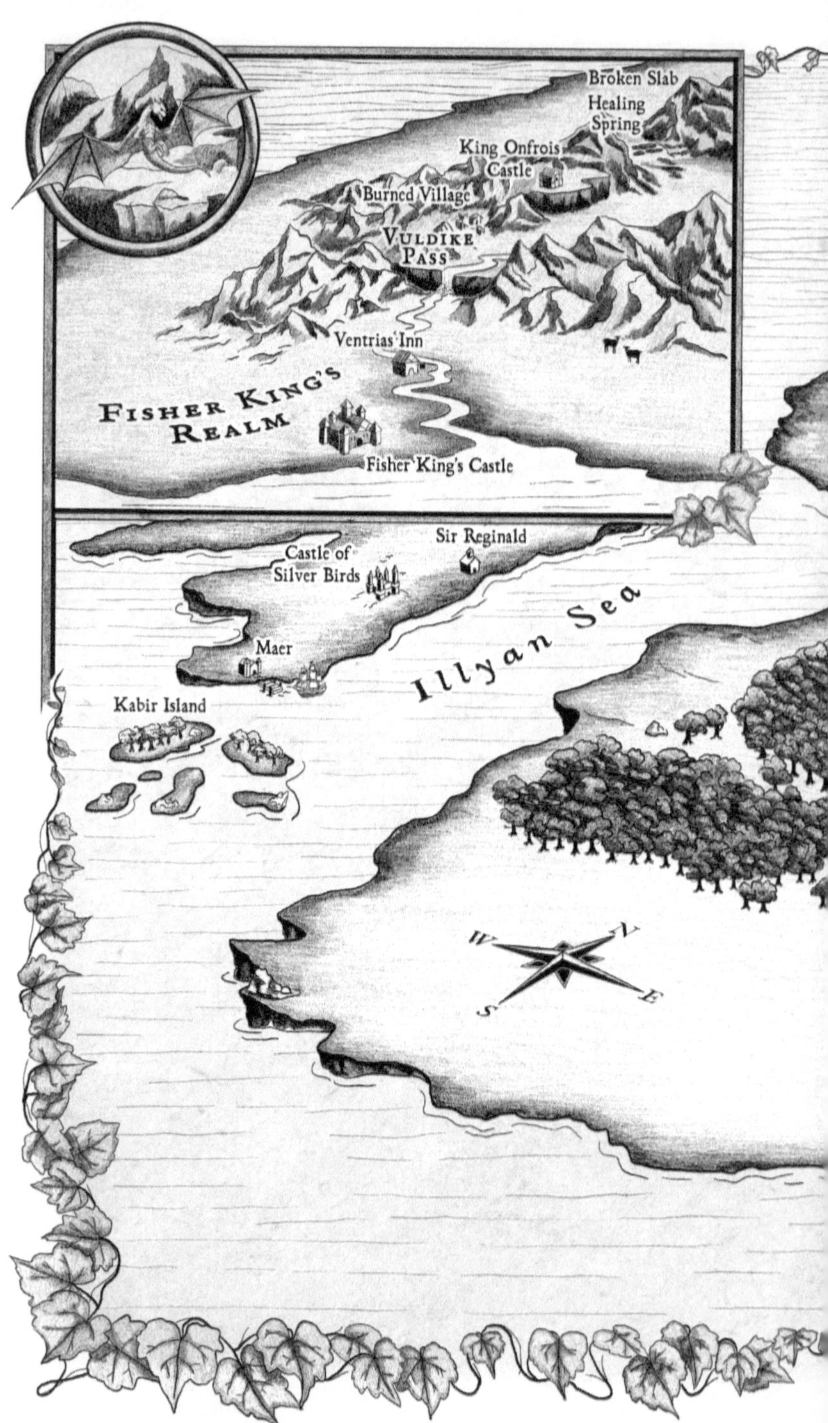

Broken Slab
Healing Spring
King Onfrois Castle
Burned Village
VULDIKE PASS
Ventrias' Inn
FISHER KING'S REALM
Fisher King's Castle
Castle of Silver Birds
Sir Reginald
Maer
Illyan Sea
Kabir Island
W N E S

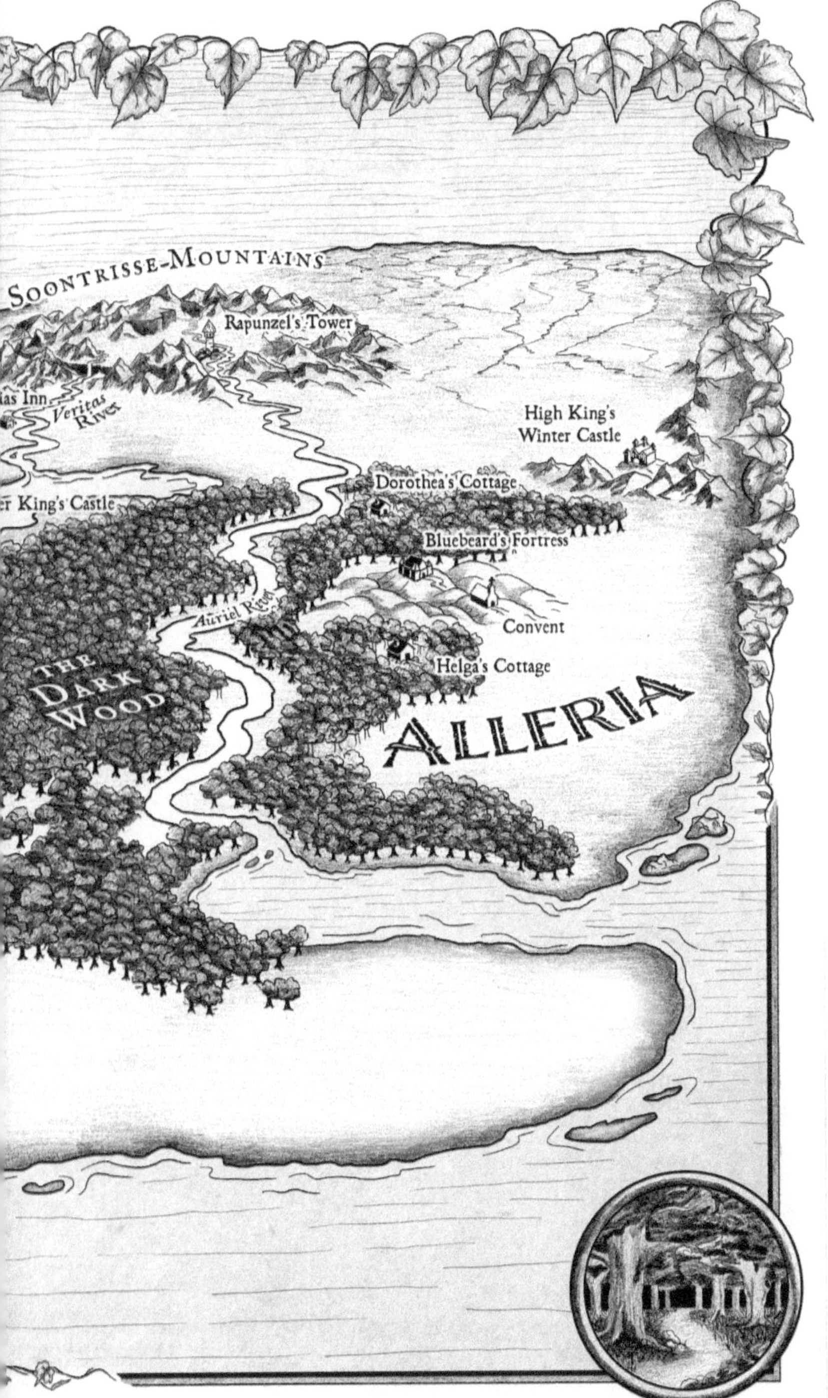

Soontrisse-Mountains
Rapunzel's Tower
Veritas River
Inn
High King's Winter Castle
King's Castle
Dorothea's Cottage
Bluebeard's Fortress
Convent
Auriel River
Helga's Cottage
THE DARK WOOD
ALLERIA

CONTENTS

THE SHAPE OF DARKNESS

There is darkness all around me except for a path of light that breaks through the inky blackness. A voice rasps, "Why? Why did you leave me?"

The witch's withered frame steps into that single sword of light.

"But you're gone—you couldn't forgive, and now you are no more."

Her cackle begins deep in her chest. "Am I really gone? There are many of us left, lurking in places you can't imagine. You try to snuff us out and we will grow stronger."

Appearing in midair, there appear three women speaking in strange tongues. My witch looks over her shoulder at them. They shimmer as she used to, changing their appearance, one becoming a dragon, another a centaur, and the last a leviathan.

"You see? I am not alone. There are others who are more powerful than even I."

My throat swells with regret. "I didn't want you to die."

"You wanted me to change, to stop being who I was. I'd rather die."

"And you did." How can I miss her? This is the woman who once imprisoned me, separated me from my love. It was she who set me on a twisted path of painful discovery. I find, though, that I do miss her. My hand reaches toward her, but she recoils in hatred.

"Get away from me! Death is better than life with a traitor like you!" She screeches, and the scream goes on and on. I watch as she breaks, leaving behind only her shattered, frozen heart.

"Rapunzel!"

My eyes pop open. My mother has her hand on my brow. I am lying on a cot in a cramped, dim room as the ground tilts from side to side. Slowly, my mind recognizes where I am: on a ship heading towards the Northlands to meet the family of my betrothed, Paul.

The nightmare begins to fade as I sit up slowly. "Did I cry out?"

My mother's face smiles sadly. "Not as loudly as last night." She asks me no questions of the darkness that still touches me at night. I could speak of it, but I don't want to. I push back the covers and begin to ready myself for the day. The captain said we should reach the shore of Trisse today, and I cannot still the anxiety that crowds my stomach. At last I will be able to begin a normal life . . . and I will finally be happy.

◌◌◌

ON SEEING the shape of the shore emerge on the horizon, I feel a throb of joy, a surge of excitement—though these come with a tremble of fear. Where am I going? What will I find when we arrive in Trisse?

"Land!" I hear the cry as the wind continues to drive us forward toward my new home.

"We'll soon be there." Paul is smiling at me. The crinkles at the corners of his eyes make me believe that happiness hovers nearby.

I can't think what to say, so I smile and nod. The idea of meeting Paul's family is a strange one. What will they think of the young woman who is responsible for the year-long absence of their son? What will they suppose to be true about our strange courtship, separation, and reunion? I have tried to not worry, but I cannot blame my fear on some enchantment. No, my days of enchantment are behind me. I must step ahead to embrace what lies before me, to discover what shape my future will take beside my beloved.

My mother is waiting next to me, and I can't help but notice that she twitches slightly before getting hold of herself. I can't blame her; she has only been in human form for a fortnight as opposed to the two decades she spent as a calico cat. I wonder briefly if she ever had fleas . . .

I hear the sailors shouting orders as we get ever closer to the Northlands. A massive anchor is lowered into the waves sloshing against the ship.

"Home!" Paul's arm is around my shoulders and he kisses me lightly on the head. A small boat is tied to the side of the ship. A sailor gets inside it while two others hold the pulley system that will allow them to lower the boat to the waters below. This smaller boat will carry us to shore while the larger ship continues on to the harbor.

I look at my mother who shakes her head a bit before she fakes a smile. It took a great deal to get her onto the ship before we left the island of Rona. Perhaps, similar to her twitching, she can't help her cat-like aversion to water. I smile with a confidence I don't feel and try to show her there is nothing to fear as I climb into the little boat. She joins me, followed by Paul. I lick my lips nervously as the boat sways while the pulleys lower it into the water. Neither I nor my companions speak. I know that my nerves keep me silent, but Paul seems ready to burst like an overripe melon in all his excitement. His eyes flicker over the landscape with anticipation.

I feel something inside me squeeze tight and I take a steadying breath. Is this joy? Is this fear? I wonder if I will ever be able to understand my emotions. They are a braided rope of tightly knotted coils, a testament to my many years as the witch's imprisoned child.

I look at my mother and smile, but the sadness inside blooms for all that I lost from the years of bitter waste. The senseless loss haunts me. Why? These two sisters, my mother and the witch—why had they not learned to trust one another, to love each other? The witch stole me and transformed my mother into a cat, punishing my mother for stealing from her garden. It grieves me that they were never able to reconcile. My mother begged forgiveness from her sister in the end, but it came too late. I'll never forget the shriveled piece of frozen heart—all that remained of the witch who had kept me as her child, captive in her tower until just a year ago.

The sound of the bottom of the boat hitting the water is louder than I imagined it would be. The waves jostle us as the sailor uses his massive arms to move the oars that pull us forward, ever closer to shore. Closer, closer, and my mother is holding my hand tighter, tighter. If she still had claws, I'm sure I'd be bleeding right now, but I press my lips to suppress my pain at her grip.

I'm surprised by how quickly we reach the sandy beach. It is littered with rocks and scruffy grass trying to survive near the lapping salt water. Paul is helping the sailor drag the boat further in so that neither my mother nor myself will get even the hem of our skirts wet by the waves' froth.

Without ceremony, Paul cradles me in his arms and kisses my cheek before carrying us to shore. "Welcome home, my love."

"Home?" I whisper, but his grin is contagious. I feel a smile taking over my face, reshaping the form of my mouth. My eyes scan the shore. The stark beauty of the enormous white cliffs stretches high above us. What is it I'm feeling? It must be something akin to belonging. This place feels oddly familiar. The waters rush up to the shore only to be pulled slowly out again, filling me with yearning. To live here with my beloved—but loss taints the moment. I don't deserve the joy being given to me.

My mother is laughing at me. "You look as bewildered as I felt on that ship." She stumbles forward slightly. "I could kiss this solid earth!"

"Oh, I think you should!" Laughter softens my sarcastic quip. I determine to stop myself from thinking morose thoughts. I don't know how, but I will make up for my flaws. I will pay back all who have helped me. Besides, I know that I am no longer alone on my journey. Paul is directing the sailor to the docks with the small boat and our belongings.

"Come," he urges before I can question why he did not take us directly to the docks. "We will journey from here on foot and stretch our legs a bit." He gestures to the steep path that will help us mount the daunting cliffs. "I have always loved this place."

His eyes are twinkling and I can't help smiling back. The view is breathtaking.

"When I was a child, I spoke like one, thought like one, and played like one. The place I loved to play best was here, on the shore where my father has many friends who allow his kingdom to trade by sea. This is my uncle's kingdom, and he and my father are great allies. My uncle's sister is my father's wife, and together their kingdoms stand stronger.

"My mother is a good woman, but very quiet. I have rarely heard her speak in my father's castle. But when she comes to the shore to visit her home, her eyes light and I hear her laugh as she seldom does in the mountains. Her heart is most alive here, so I would share with you this place before we journey further."

Disappointment fills me as I glance back at the horizon, where the bright blue of the sky meets the deep green of the sea. "So, this is not your home?"

"No, Rapunzel, this *is* my home, though not the kingdom of my birth. My uncle's wife died several years ago and he never remarried. He is without a son. I will inherit his kingdom on his death."

I shake my head, thinking back over what I learned about his family as we prepared to travel. "But I thought you said you had an older brother."

"I do, and he will inherit my father's throne, but I will inherit my uncle's as the next nearest male relative."

I shake my head slightly. "But then I will be—"

"You will be queen." Paul holds out a hand to help me up the last steep stretch. I climb up to a plateau covered by a thick carpet of bright green grass.

My mother comes up behind us, and Paul helps her as well. She stares at me, silently, her large green eyes unblinking. My mouth is dry and I take in a deep breath, but it does nothing to calm me.

Paul frowns as he looks at me. "You don't seem—"

"Give her time," my mother interrupts, placing a hand on Paul's muscled forearm. "She needs a moment to think this through. Becoming a queen is something strange for someone raised as our Rapunzel was."

Paul nods his head, but his shoulders drop. I can't look him in the eye, so I look around me. To the west, where Rona lies, the sun is slowly lowering. It is a few hours till sunset, and I hope that is long enough for us to reach the docks.

During my time on Rona, when I was bewitched into a betrothal to the manipulative Prince Edmund, I wrestled with the thought of being queen. As my feet travel on the white path, I can't help wondering: did I not want to be queen, or did I simply not want to be Edmund's queen? I waffle with uncertainty. I fear the doubt that plagued my relationship with Edmund may plague my betrothal to Paul.

OLD FRIENDS

_P_aul is right. Walking all the way to the docks refreshes us. The seagulls caw loudly as they pick at the wriggling fish that are being brought in. The salty smell of sea creatures is ripe in the warm sun. I wish I could pinch my nose, but I don't want to be rude. My mother, though, actually licks her lips as she leaves us, stalking over to a stall, her shoulders hunched up to her ears. She quietly creeps up on people gathering to haggle over the last of the day's catch.

"Ca—Mother?" I call. When her feline tendencies emerge, I find it difficult to not address her as "Cat," as I did for so long.

Paul chuckles and runs after her. "Where we are going, there will be plenty of fish to eat. Trust me!"

Her head jerks, and she blinks, as though coming out of some sort of trance. "I'm sorry! Of course."

"Mother"—I frown—"I thought you would have had your fill of fish while on board!"

"One can never have enough fish." Her eyes glance back at the stall, but she reins herself in. We follow as Paul leads us straight to a tavern. It is not the first tavern in the port city that I have seen, but he seems to prefer this one. I look up as we approach and stare at the painted sun swinging on a sign jutting out above the large dark door.

As Paul ushers us inside, the yeasty smells of fresh bread and ale intermingle with that of the baked fish. It is strange and wonderful. I am not overly excited about more fish, but days of stale bread and watery ale have left me yearning for this treat of fresh food. I feel my face grow warm when my stomach gurgles.

"It seems your mother is not the only one who is hungry." Paul's smile is wide and my heart squeezes as I think of getting to enjoy him for the rest of my life. He leads us to one of only two empty tables. This tavern is well-loved. I notice that most of the people here have that "Northland" look about them—they are tall, like Paul, but even more fair-skinned, and their bodies are more slender. They have a distinct way of holding themselves: erect, shoulders back, chin up, as though they have never bent forward in their lives. One might think them standoffish, but upon meeting them, they soon thaw with a smile.

We have just sat down when a young maid comes to our table to greet us. She speaks in the Northland language, the one I was raised with. "What can I br—"

"Paul!" A melodious voice breaks through the sounds of the tavern's hungry patrons. A plump woman, who looks Allerian and is probably a bit older than my mother, comes from the back of the building carrying a pitcher of ale. She is dressed in a simple brown cotehardie and a surcoat that is partially covered by a worn apron. Her white-blonde hair is uncovered in the way of Northland women, and her eyes are pale blue. Her skin is flushed from working near the fires, reminding me how hot a kitchen can get. As soon as she weaves her way among the tables to reach us, she sets down the pitcher, spilling a bit. She steps forward with a broad smile on her face, her arms outstretched. "Our Paul! Where have you been? We have missed you! Why did you not come for the past two summers?" She embraces Paul as though she were a close relative.

"Thora, meet Rapunzel, my betrothed." I flush as the woman curtsies. Strange how free I feel when Paul calls me his betrothed, so unlike how I felt when Edmund would speak of me. I smile at her familiar greeting of Paul; it speaks well, both of him and the woman. But before I can blink, she has filled large tankards of ale and brought hot bread which fills me with warmth.

My mother's eyes catch every movement. She is ill at ease in the company of so many. I wonder how she will fare in the Great Hall of the king. I notice Thora as she directs maids nearby, then comes to stand by Paul, delivering the baked fish herself. I take the first bite out of politeness and find to my relief that the seafood is as good as I've had anywhere. I eat with relish, once again glad to be off the ship.

"So, are you the reason he has not come to see us in so long?" I glance up, astonished by her accusing tone, and find to my relief that she is laughing. "We have long prayed for this day! It must be quite the tale to have taken Paul from us for two summers' time. I thought for a while he was simply out hunting—"

"You know how I do love a good hunt!" Paul laughs around a mouthful of the well-seasoned fish. I do notice my mother has finished her own and begins stealing off my trencher.

"—but for two summers? Surely the Fisher King had something to say about that!"

"I have yet to see my uncle."

A shadow crosses her features. "Oh, I thought you would know . . ."

The corners of Paul's mouth pull down. "Know what, Thora?"

"It is—he is much changed, they say. But surely your father knows that—and you should, too." She's now frowning, perplexed by my love's ignorance. "It was partly why I was surprised we hadn't seen you."

"I have not seen my father, either, in nearly a year's time."

"Oh, dear."

"We haven't fallen out—it simply took me a year to gain Rapunzel's hand in marriage."

Well, that's an interesting way to put it, I think to myself.

"What is wrong with—"

"I'm sorry, my lord, I shouldn't say any more. Let your uncle explain. Please, finish your meal." She leaves us then, a backward glance over her shoulder revealing fresh wrinkles of worry on her pink face.

The remainder of our meal is eaten in sedate silence. Paul chews his food quickly, wanting to be gone. Mother and I follow his lead and take in only what we need to be on our way as soon as can be.

THE FISHER KING

*E*ntering the castle is a blur. We are rushed into the king's sick chamber where two long windows are open to circulate the air for the invalid. The king is propped up in bed, but still he manages to look quite noble. He is wearing a robe of royal blue, his kingdom's color, which matches his eyes. His dark hair, I can tell by the little that peeks out beneath his embroidered white bed cap, is greying. To the king's right, next to the grand bed, there is a small table covered by a golden fishing net, on top of which his crown rests. A golden trident stands propped against the table instead of a scepter, completing the ensemble. I imagine the man before me—hale, standing aboard a fishing vessel, using his trident and net to bring in large sea monsters. I should find it difficult to picture him this way, given his emaciated state, but there is something about the way he resists slumping. The jut of his chin that tells me this man is still a warrior and far from finished with his battle.

"So, you have returned to us at last, lost nephew."

"I would have come sooner if I could have, your Majesty. I had no idea—"

But the king stops any regret or pity with a raised hand. "We have heard from your father of your disappearance, how your mysterious hunting activities had ensnared you. You've caused no end of worry, more for us than for your father. After all, you will inherit our throne."

"You are right to speak to me so. I hope that my absence did not cause—"

But the king chortles at this and then begins to cough. A demure maid steps forward at once to pour him some water from a lovely golden pitcher resting on the small table to the king's left. His breathing wheezes, and then settles at last. We all wait in silence. If he were not a king, I would say that he now smirks as he resumes dialoguing with his nephew. "You are of great importance, it is true, but you did not cause this." He gestures to himself, but still will not speak aloud of what ails him. The king shakes his head. "We may have blamed your absence for prolonging it, but now we know differently. We suppose you have not seen your father. Surely the king would have said something."

"No, I was going there next to ask his—"

The king raises a hand as his dark brows lower. He now fixes his gaze first on me and then on my mother, who I pray will not twitch. "We see, your mysterious disappearance has borne fruit, has it not? Whom have you brought with you into our presence?"

"This is my betrothed, Rapunzel, and her mother, Katterina."

"You have become betrothed without first seeking the blessing of the throne?"

"I have."

The king nods thoughtfully, but he is still frowning,

contemplating I know not what. Did he have his own plans for the future queen of his kingdom? The thought stuns me and I cannot help the shudder that passes through me. Though the likelihood of becoming queen has frightened me, living without Paul is not something I am willing to do.

The moment is burdened with expectation when the king resumes speaking. He takes several drinks from his shining goblet and at last hands it back to the waiting maid. He then turns his eyes on Paul. "You have never been an impetuous man, though we all know that, in the matters of love, even the most sturdy of us falter. Still, we would like to trust your judgment." He looks again at me. "We will have to acquaint ourselves with you, dear lady. You do understand, don't you, that you must suit the needs of both the future king as well as the kingdom?"

I cannot speak for the dryness of my mouth, but I give a low bow to acquiesce.

He is still staring at me when I rise, his eyes narrowing somewhat. The gaze that takes me in is not displeased, simply assessing. "Well, you will have great opportunity to prove yourself in the coming days."

"Your Majesty?" Paul has been quietly taking our exchange in but must feel the need to speak at last.

"We know that you must be anxious to return home to your father, to explain your disappearance and resume your life—but as you can see, your future is quickly approaching. We have need of you, and though it will take you into the mountains, you will not have long to tarry with your family. But first—we have business to discuss with you about the kingdom you are to gain."

"I would like to think that you know that *this* is my home. Of course I would like to see my father and the rest of my family. I know I should speak of what has kept me from them for so long and introduce them to Rapunzel and her mother. But whatever must be done for this kingdom will be my highest priority."

The king nods and a muscle jerks in his cheek. Is that another hint of a smile? A small murmur of pride in his nephew? I am tempted to like the man from these small gestures of confidence. "You will do well. You know your place, as you always have. The people have long been your main concern, which is why your absence was so unexpected."

"I would like to explain—"

Quite suddenly, the king droops, his head falling back against the bright white cushions propping him up. "We will speak . . . later." He uses the last bit of his energy to direct us away as the maid rushes forward to help him lie back down. I look away from the monarch to save his pride.

⸙

A SERVANT LEADS us to our separate chambers. Paul had made arrangements before leaving the ship that his mare and our things would be brought from the docks to the castle. He smiles at me and wishes me good night before the servant ushers him to his bedchamber down the hall. I take comfort knowing he is nearby.

I look around the room. It has a fireplace to keep the chill out of the grey stones. Nearby, the huge bed tempts me to rest, adorned with luxurious blue bedding and curtains. I suppose my mother is not as tired as I am. I watch as she opens the window, looking down into the courtyard. Servants are scuttling over the cobblestones as they finish their chores before the last bit of light dwindles in the sky.

"Paul's uncle is an interesting man."

"Indeed."

I am glad that the maid who has come into the chambers to wait on us is quiet. She fills the water basin that rests to the right of the bed. "May I get you something to eat?"

"What is your name?"

She looks surprised by my inquiry. "Ingrid." I blink as she gives an awkward squat. I wonder if she meant to curtsy.

"Ingrid, thank you so much for your kindness, but I think all we need is some wine to drink before bed."

"At once, my lady." She curtsies for sure this time and closes the door behind her quietly.

I turn to my mother, still entranced by the comings and goings outside. I stand beside her and take note of her attentive eyes.

"Mother—" my voice sounds strained "—do you see things the same way anymore?"

She turns to look at me with her head tilted slightly.

I moisten my lips and try again. "I mean, can you remember what life was like before you were feline?"

She nods.

"And did being Cat change how you see the world?"

She turns from me and looks down below us. "Everything we go through changes us. We can't ever see things the way we once did. I suppose normality is out of reach for some of us. I was a greedy young woman, Rapunzel. I had everything—a husband who loved me, a child within my womb—but I was hungry for more. Why did I want what my sister had?"

The moment hangs.

"You're not that same woman anymore."

She reaches out with her long, delicate fingers and cups my face with both hands. "I hope not. When I was Cat, I saw how empty want leaves you. There is no blessing appreciated, no love for the God who made us."

I've never heard her speak of God before. "And now?"

"I have many regrets, but I have grace as well. Grace is a strange thing, unearned, undeserved. When I look down at these servants rushing about, I see opportunity, I see purpose. Being Cat changed me forever, but . . . I feel as though I am still transforming, altering into someone different. Not Cat, but not the woman I was, either. I don't really know who I am." She lets her hands drop away from me, but I catch and hold them.

"I know. We will discover who you are—together."

"I can never thank you enough for forgiving me, for bringing me with you."

I look away from her unblinking eyes. "I don't feel I really know where we are going or what we will find along the way, but I am glad we are together."

A stillness settles over us even as we ready ourselves for bed. The young servant who comes to attend us seems to sense this and does not intrude on the peace that covers us like a blanket. I climb onto the high bed I will share with my mother. I fall asleep to the sound of her soft breathing, which becomes a rhythmic humming snore.

SEARCHING

The darkness pulls me into itself even as my eyes close. My witch appears, and beside her, the others I saw with her before. Their hair is floating about them as they levitate, and they look as though they are floating in water—but they aren't. Voices rise as they chant again in that strange tongue. I've heard it before. It was the one language my witch would never teach me, though I would hear her speaking in it as she gathered some of her smelly herbs.

My witch looks young, face unlined and her hair dark like my mother's. As she sits at the feet of the others, they begin their transformation. The witch joins the chanting, and she alters. Youth is stripped away and she is old and brittle, hiding her beauty behind a mask of hatred. Suddenly she turns and screams at me, but I manage to wake without crying, for once.

All is quiet except for the sound of my mother's soft snores and my labored breath. It is that strange time of night right before first light. I won't be able to return to sleep, so with soft movements I dress myself in what I hope is my favorite cotehardie of emerald, over which I slip a sideless surcoat the color of pale leaves. I slip out the door with a candle and begin to wind my way through the castle. I have told myself before that this is not the wisest thing to do when visiting a castle. After all, I am a guest . . . but I can't seem to stop myself from exploring.

Most castles are built around the Great Hall where the kings or lords sup, and I find my way there. It is a massive room, one of the finest I have ever seen. I judge it equal to that of the High King in Alleria, where I stayed while discovering what had happened to enchant his twelve bratty princesses. The walls of grey stone are covered in the royal-blue banners embroidered with golden tritons, hanging lengthwise on the opposite ends of the hall. There are long windows that allow in the light of the breaking dawn. There is a colossal tapestry denoting the history of the kingdom behind the raised platform where I imagine the king sits when he is well enough to dine and hold court.

The tapestry spans the length of the mammoth table. For the first time, I see the shape of our large island as though I am a bird looking at the land from up in the clouds. It looks like a woman leaning her head forward toward the Illyan Sea that separates her from the smaller island of Rona. Trisse, the great port city of the Fisher King's realm, rests on the Northland's "chin" and provides the best access to the Soontrisse Mountains in the Northlands. Hovering over the sea, four people are depicted, with great armies lined up in the middle of our island, accentuating the boundary line between the countries of Alleria and the Northlands. Hooded cloaks are draped over the hovering people, who are each holding out their right hand, pushing their palms flat out into the air in front of them. They are pushing in the same direction as though to move an invisible wall. One of these is a giant of a man, while the other three are women. Though their faces are not clear to me from this distance, I feel a shiver along my spine. A hand touches my shoulder and I yelp.

"Why aren't you asleep?" Paul is behind me and I throw my arms around him. Perhaps the nightmare has clung to me more than I thought it had. "What is this about?"

I'm surprised and ashamed of the tears that I find wetting my face. "I don't know, I was just frightened."

"And you're out of your room because . . .?"

"I—I keep having these strange dreams. Lately, they have grown worse. I can't sleep after they wake me." He looks as though he will ask me more questions, so I take the opportunity to distract him.

"Why are you up this early?"

"I am often up early. I find it hard to sleep for very long. To tell the truth, my uncle's ill health disturbs me."

I nod and then glance up at the wall. "What is happening in this tapestry? I don't understand."

He looks at me in surprise. "Sometimes I forget what you were never taught of the world outside of what the witch wanted you to know. Forgive me.

"It was the War of Sorcery, fought when my father was young. There was a powerful wizard called the Grand Sorcerer—" he gestures to the malevolent character floating between the women "—who had three daughters. He was born the third prince in the kingdom between our lands." He points at the line separating the Northlands and Alleria, a ridged edge of two lines of warriors facing one another: spears and swords on horseback on one side, with a line of wizards and witches holding their hands aloft on the other. "It is said that his family intended him for the church when he was young, but he hated the monks who helped raise him. He discovered sorcery when he ran away into the Dark Wood. Hating God as he did, it was easy for him to take his stand against the Church when they condemned sorcery."

"Do all who practice magic stand in opposition to God?"

"I believe there are those who mistakenly practice it, but I have always been told that God clearly hates it, that it is dangerous for man to try to manipulate the supernatural. To do so opens the door to evil things in the spirit realm."

I shiver once more, now thinking of the magic I have encountered. Haven't I been touched by such evil things?

Paul continues, "He was furious with the Church for condemning sorcery. He amassed armies to fight against the kingdoms of the islands."

"How does one fight a sorcerer?"

"Legions of warrior-monks came forth and fought— from the kingdoms of Rona, the Eastern Ports, Alleria, and the Northlands."

I thought of all the priests and monks I had chanced to encounter. "I did not know there were monks who were trained to fight."

The smile on my beloved's face deepens. "They are quite good with a sword or a staff, many with a bow. I was trained by one here, myself. The sorcerers would rain down incantations while the monks would rush them while citing scripture and calling on God's name. Many lost their lives in the battles that erupted all over the two islands. The chaos was dramatic. Peace-loving people found themselves pulled to one side or the other because they loved a sister who practiced sorcery or because they had given a son to the church. What we did not know till later was that most of the turmoil was caused by the shape-shifting daughters of the Grand Sorcerer. They were everywhere at once, sewing discord, inciting rebellion, causing neighbors to burn the crops of neighbors. Starvation was imminent in all but the coastlands."

"What could justify such destruction? Why would anyone want such death?"

"Power. He wanted to be the ruler of it all, and he nearly was. There would be no peace, no one left alive except those who practiced sorcery. During the war, he ravaged the minds of the generals, who took to killing whole villages of women and children. The people would seek sanctuary in the village church, and the armies would set them on fire."

"I don't understand." I'm repulsed by the thought of such violence.

He looks at me and tucks a loose lock of golden hair up into my wimple. "If you understood it, I would worry. You don't hunger after power. At the height of the war, the daughters turned against their father. Some say he was abusive with his power, others say the women became greedy. At the time they struck him down, he released a curse on them, separating them forever and limiting their powers."

"They are still alive?"

"Some say so, though they haven't been seen for many years."

"You said the father was struck down."

"Yes—while his back was turned as he cast a powerful incantation, his daughters each took their enchanted knives and together stabbed him in the back as they chanted."

"Were they trying to curse him?"

"They were trying to kill him. Good thing, too, for their little rebellion cost them the war."

"And the people?" I think through my time wandering through the heart of Alleria, and later all over Rona. Why had I not seen devastation? Where were all the burned churches? I couldn't fathom how many years it would take to recuperate from such damage.

"Blessings from heaven poured forth. The next several harvests were miraculously good across the islands, and the kingdoms of Ethrid sent aid. The people were able to rebuild their villages and livestock, my father told me. Though lives had been lost, peace returned and the kings established a new order to rule the islands."

"Ah, yes, I have met the High King."

Paul laughs. "He is a bit of a disappointment these days, but I have been told that his father ruled well and inspired loyalty. It is hard to live up to the reputation of a great father. When the High King holds court in the Eastern Ports every few summers, he sobers for a short time and makes sound judgments. Personally, I do not care for him, but he is the High King and we hope one day he will have an heir that will resemble his father."

I shake my head. I have met the man who may become the next High King, and there was little to recommend him.

OUR TALE

e are once again in the Fisher King's chambers, but this time he has had ornate mahogany chairs brought in on which we sit, facing His Majesty. No longer as pale as he was the evening before, I can imagine how far he must have declined by the way Paul suppresses a frown when we first enter. A steward brings us bowls of cooked grain with pears. Evidently, we are to break fast together. The maid that was waiting on His Majesty the night before now hands a bowl to the king and holds his goblet for him, exchanging bowl and goblet anytime he gestures for it. There is such a tenderness in how she looks on him that I think, how wonderful to inspire such loyalty in a servant. He smiles at her, then redirects all his attention to Paul.

"Yesterday evening, you left before explaining what kept you from your duties these past two summers. There is now time for you to tell me."

Paul swallows and places his bowl in his lap. "I was out hunting last summer, just before the time I usually come to visit you. You'll remember that two springs ago, you gave leave for me to travel to the council in the Eastern Ports to represent my father and yourself, as my brother's wife, Aalis, was having trouble with bearing the heir. When I returned mid-summer and gave the message to my father, Princess Aalis seemed better and the child was soon to be born. As you had sent word to come once the child had been christened, I made ready to travel so I could leave at once. But waiting grated on me, so I spent my days hunting."

The Fisher King gives a grunt of approval. "Of course you did."

"I am a hunter by nature, am I not?"

The king laughs, and I am relieved there is no sound of wheezing in it this time.

Paul smiles and his shoulders relax as he resumes his story. "While out hunting, I became lost, caught in a mist in the wood that led me to a field of sunflowers. Though it was dusk, I found the buck I had killed, but I heard something as I approached a broad wall that enclosed a tower."

"What was it?"

"An old woman's voice. I stayed very still and watched as she emerged from the tower and slipped down a rope. The rope traveled back inside, and I supposed the old woman to have left the enclosure by a door on the other side. Soon after, a maid came to the window, and as darkness fell, her voice filled the air with song. I walked all along the outer perimeter of the wall, but could find no opening, no door. Still, the song went on and on. I knew I needed to return to my father's home. But I stayed till the maid finally stopped singing and had blown her candle out."

His Majesty is leaning forward a bit, a knowing smile dimpling his clean-shaven face. "You went back."

At this Paul frowns. "I tried to, but the path eluded me.

It took a week before I decided to blindfold myself and my mare. When I did, I felt the cool mist. It was as though a hand gently pulled us forward. I smelled the nutty fragrance of sunflowers and I could hear her voice singing again. I just listened that night, but the next time I returned, I grew impatient."

"A dangerous thing for a hunter."

Paul has forgotten the food resting on his lap in the telling of our tale. "I no longer felt like a hunter. It was as though I were rescuing a wounded animal who had become caught in a trap."

"You were the singer?" The king cuts me with his gaze.

"I was, Your Majesty."

"And was the tower a trap for you or a trap for my nephew?"

"Your Majesty, if I may?" My mother begs permission to speak. The king gives a tiny nod of his head, and she proceeds. "Long ago, I hurt my sister. Had she been an ordinary woman, we would have simply hated each other and taught our families to spurn each other's company. But she was a witch, and she exacted a heavy price for my sin. She took Rapunzel, my daughter, and eventually locked her up in a tower, casting a spell on the fields around her."

The king gives my mother a strange look. "And she did nothing to you?"

"She turned me into a cat and later killed my husband —but I'm not a cat anymore."

The dimple in his cheek appears again. "I can see that."

My mother flushes at his words.

We remain silent, letting the king contemplate as he sips from his cup. He exchanges it for food, takes a bite, and nods thoughtfully at his nephew to proceed.

"I tried to set Rapunzel free, but the witch caught us

first. She sent Rapunzel out into the world, unable to settle anywhere. She spent the past year moving and roaming, unable to make a home. I lost my memory and found myself on Rona, serving a lord."

There is a space of hush. Our story sounds ludicrous when it is spoken aloud. Only in living it can one believe the strange things that occurred.

"Rapunzel—" the king addresses me after taking another swallow of wine "—what happened to resolve these matters?"

"I discovered Paul in the Great Hall of a lord in Rona. He did not recognize me. That is—at first, he didn't. After a time, he sought me out. And the witch, she died. My mother was transformed back into herself. And then . . . well, Paul asked me to be his wife and brought me here." I swallow the lump of fear lodged in my throat. I know it sounds all chopped up. I take a deep breath, try to think coherently. "But I understand if a maid like myself is unacceptable as queen. I have led a very strange and disorderly life."

Paul reaches to hold my hand, and I am grateful for the comfort as we wait in silence. The king chews and then takes another draught before commenting.

"Your life is the kind of life a jester might make into an entertaining song." He seems to be smirking again. "Most of us lead quiet lives. Would you have preferred that, Rapunzel?"

"I would have liked the choice. I think now—"

"We are afraid that what you have to endure will continue to confound that dream of normalcy, my dear." He gestures toward the wall where a few guards stand motionless, awaiting his command. "I believe you know this man?"

A man steps forward and I blink to make sense of the

image. My eyes must be lying to me! Before me stands not a guard, but a dark-eyed jester. He bounds forward and handsprings toward me. Paul rises, stepping in front of me. The sharp metal of his sword zips through the air making a clanging sound, clashing with the metallic crunching noise of the jester's chain mail. He hits with the flat of the sword and doesn't harm the man. It is just a warning to keep back.

The fool claps. "He has good reflexes, Your Majesty!"

Paul doesn't relax his stance or remove his gaze from the man. "Do you know this man, Rapunzel?"

"I met him only last summer while on Rona." I turn my head towards the fool. "But what are you doing here?"

"I've left one castle for another, you see? Adventure beckoned when I glimpsed a bit of your coming story, my dear. I traveled the seas despite the threat of pirates. I see that you made it safely across as well."

The king laughs. "You silly fool, pirates like to roam closer to the Eastern Ports. You were in no danger!" He smiles at us as he says, "I sent for him. Amis is more than he seems."

The jester, our fool Amis, nods. "The Lady Rapunzel will understand that, Your Majesty, she is ever so much more than she seems."

My chest feels heavy at his words, and Paul chances a glance at me before addressing the king again. "What is he going on about, Your Majesty?"

But the Fisher King smiles in a weary sort of way. "Paul, you are so serious." He begins to cough. "I am sorry, I am tired now and must rest. Don't worry, tonight all will be revealed. I don't mean to keep you in suspense . . ."

"No?" Paul cocks his head.

"Well, maybe a little bit. After two years away, it is my turn, after all. I will say this: it is a serious business, but

Amis can spin it into a tale that gives me hope. And right now, Paul, I'm in desperate need of hope."

He lifts his hand with that same gesture of dismissal. He slouches against the cushions again as the burden of what we don't yet know weighs on him. The maid grabs his goblet, which is not quite empty. She deftly lays aside his things to help him back in bed while we are once more ushered out of his presence. Will we never discover what it is that troubles the king?

I have never been a guest in a castle quite like this one. It is unusual, as it stands on top of the bluff, overlooking the white cliffs that face the Illyan Sea. Unlike where our boat let us out, the sea has eroded all of the shore up to this cliff. After we are dismissed from the king's presence, my mother excuses herself to spend some time alone in our chambers. Amis has stayed behind with the king, so Paul and I walk together by ourselves. I am pleased when Paul takes my hand. "Come with me, I want to show you something."

I think for a moment he is stealing me away for a kiss. When we were getting along, Edmund would do that as often as I allowed, and sometimes even when I didn't want him to. But Paul has only kissed me once when we were alone. Perhaps that is the proper way of things, but my mind worries over the thought that he does not desire me as I desire him. Silly, worrisome girl! I must not let my emotions carry me away.

He leads me through many hallways, and I wonder at the structure of the fortress. Built of grey stone, it is chilly, so I am grateful for the many fires burning cheerfully in several of the rooms we pass by. While the numerous hallways seem well planned and straight, as we reach the back part of the castle there is something twisting at work. I feel as though I am losing my sense of where we are in the overall structure, and I cast a suspicious glance about me. I am quite good with directions unless magic is involved to befuddle me. "Where are we?"

"We're almost there." Paul's voice is calm and settles most of my fears. This isn't magic—this is strange and ancient architecture. We come to the bottom of a dark staircase, and Paul holds out the candle he has had the foresight to bring with him. Without a word, we wind our way up steep stairs, and he sets down the candle on the landing before opening the door to a bright, spacious chamber. In the center of the room is a massive pit laid with fire and a flue overhead directing the smoke to the chimney above. Even with the flue, I can smell something harsh. The wood has been oiled with something smelly to prolong the flame. The circular room, a tower, really, is made up of archways facing the sea on every side except the one we have come from. I did not realize we were up so much higher than the rest of the castle! I hear the ferocious sound of water below us, spitting its anger in a roaring foam as it beats against the rocks in wave after tumultuous wave. If my hair were not concealed beneath my cap and wimple, my curls would be flying about my head. I feel a smile stretch my mouth as I rush from window to window looking out. "What is this place?" I nearly shout to be heard above the noise.

"It is a lighthouse, quite old, older than the rest of the castle." Paul has to raise his voice as well. "It has been here from ancient times, guiding and directing our ancestors to shore safely, keeping them from hitting the cliffs of Trisse."

My mind remembers the tapestry I saw this morning. Are we on the corner of the "chin" of the Northlands? I stare down and watch the waves erupting along the dazzling white cliffs. I tremble at the thought of our ship encountering bad weather with no light to guide us away from such a fate.

"Does it burn constantly?"

"Yes, and at night or during a storm, there is a guard assigned to keep watch over the light. In Rona, I saw a tower that had glass windows to keep the gales from blowing out the flames, I wonder . . ." I can see his mind is contemplating how to better run the kingdom once it is under his rule. Such an undertaking would take a great deal of work and money, but I have seen nothing to suggest that this kingdom is lacking, either. I wonder at the thought of inheriting such a gift, but we don't want that yet. There must be a way to help the king recover and live for many more years. Paul and I need time to grow together and learn our roles. I feel ashamed at my thoughts. I hope I don't simply want the king to recover for selfish reasons.

"This was my favorite room as a child. When my mother and I would come to visit, I would pester her with question after question, all about the castle and the sea. I asked why the sea was big, why it was green, why it was so rough. Even before we greeted the king, I would beg to go see the 'big fire room' before we did anything else." He seems lost in an ocean of memories.

"You never spoke of the sea when you visited me in my tower." I look at him, wondering at this side of his life, this secret he had kept. In my landlocked tower, would I have been able to comprehend the notion of such a large body of water? I had read a story about a man making his way home across waters and encountering difficulties, but my imaginings were nothing compared to reality.

"I never told you I was the son of a king, either."

"No," I say, frowning, "you never did. Why?"

His gaze is direct, his hazel eyes suddenly as green as the sea below. He leads me out of the room as though this conversation must not be shouted. We stand on the landing, the sound of the crashing waves now behind the door. "At first, I didn't know what to tell you—I doubted you were real. And as I became convinced you were real, I discovered that you liked me for myself."

I give him what must be a strange look, so he elaborates.

"You weren't like the preening maids at court who fawned over me when they realized I, too, would inherit a kingdom. I had watched my brother, Roland, struggle with whom to wed. He was never quite certain whether his betrothed loved him or the throne. Not that it would have changed things. The match was decided between Aalis's father and mine. Still, the night before they wed, Roland drank too freely and told me how he wished he knew for certain if she cared for him. If they were peasants and he had little, would she still want to share his home and bed?"

I blink at Paul. "You worried I would only want to be queen?"

His laugh is hoarse. "And now I worry you won't want to be queen at all."

I must look elsewhere, and so my gaze lights on the dance of the small flame burning the wick of the candle he has picked up from the landing.

"You were going to be his queen—Edmund's."

I shake my head, wishing to erase that part of my life. "I was under the power of his wish."

"You traveled with him and his parents for the summer. You viewed his kingdom, the entire island, and—"

"And I found *you* and told him I couldn't marry him,

not to be his queen or his wife. I could never be anyone's wife but yours."

There is a hollow here; the question must be answered. "But to be my wife means you must also be my queen. Is that what you want?"

"I'm not even sure I will be a good wife. How can I become a queen?"

"Just as I will become a king. We will learn how together."

I want to believe him, I want to agree. "We don't even have permission—not your father's or your uncle's! What if they decide against—"

"They will have no reason to say 'no' to you. I know for certain that my father does not concern himself in my match."

"No?"

"No, he has my brother, and he has long directed my loyalties here. My uncle seems to look on you with curiosity and—I think—favor."

"I hope so." I breathe.

"You do?"

"Yes."

"So . . . you will be my queen?"

"I will try my best."

THE QUEST

*A*mis enjoys making a good show of his entrance. We have just been seated again when he bounds into the king's chambers. Though he can't do as many flips as he might if we were eating in the Great Hall, he makes do with the space allotted. He is not wearing the chain mail he was wearing earlier, but is now dressed in the royal blue of the Fisher King. I wonder how on earth he is keeping his bright blue jester's cap upon his head while he is jumping about.

The king claps even with his diminished energy. "Amis, we are glad you have come to entertain us."

"I am grateful for the opportunity and all that lies before us." The man is literally bounding to tell his tale, but the king holds him off by holding up a hand.

"Before I let you begin—Paul, I believe you remember Brother Jacob?"

Paul stands straight and tall as a man approaches. I assume from his dark skin tone that he hails originally from the Eastern Ports. But the man is not wearing the common coarse brown robes of a monk. Instead, he wears the blues of the Fisher King under thick chain mail, while his brown tonsure gleams as it reflects the light streaming in from the window. The men grasp arms and clap each other's back. "It is good to see you again!" Paul says.

"I have prayed for your safe return, your Highness."

Paul's stands stiff as though being inspected, but his eyes are alight at the sight of the man old enough to be his father.

The king regains our attention. "Over the summer, Amis returned to the home of his birth to find us."

Paul surprises me when he interrupts. "Why would a fool leave the hearth of his lord?"

The king laughs. "It is true that most jesters stay at one hearth, loyal to one lord—but when one has the gift of a prophet, one must travel to deliver his message. Amis' father did the same when Amis was younger and still learning his craft. He traveled from our kingdom to Maer's port to advise them of the coming famine in Rona. Who knew that a fool could be the wisest advisor? Trade agreements helped the entire island survive, if you remember your history."

A gift of prophecy in a fool? He stares at me until I look at him and he waggles thick, dark eyebrows. If he is a prophet, his mirth defies the gravity of his words.

"Last summer I met the Lady Rapunzel, though she was betrothed to someone else at the time."

"Is that so?" At this, the king furrows his brow.

Amis intercedes, "She was under a spell, but is now free. She has been freed in order to help us now." I remember the words with which he confused me last summer, that I would save the people of my kingdom.

"So, my prophet, you think she is part of this? What say you, Brother Jacob?"

"Though you know I have difficulty with the word of a

fool—" I cannot tell if Brother Jacob is as stern as he seems "—I know that we have agreed thus far. I believe these women may be able to help us, though I wish it were not so."

The king nods, face still drawn in concentration. "With Brother Jacob's help, we have begun to discern what is causing the illness throughout the Northland kingdoms."

"There are others who are ill?" Paul is as lost as I am.

"It has taken time for us to discover this, but yes. There is not a king who has not grown ill or died."

"My father?"

"Your father is affected, though not dead, thank God. Amis?"

The man I know as the jester steps forward, but he takes out no objects to juggle, no lute to strum. He lifts his high voice and begins to sing the tale of a king who goes out to fish in his kingdom by the sea. The sovereign greets the common people and brings in a good catch, but he grows weary before rowing to shore. Weakness has been sapping his strength over the summer and now it seems to have caught him at last. His man-at-arms rows him back and returns him to the castle, but despite many consultations, no apothecary can cure him. Rumors begin to drift toward the seashore, carried on the wind from the kingdoms of the Northlands. Other kings have grown ill, some to the point of death. Whispers begin to multiply. Could it be sorcery?

A monk at his prayers is frustrated beyond endurance. He travels beyond the foothills to the pass. After days of fasting and prayer, he hears the voice of the Lord and knows what he must do. He returns to the king. There is a quest ahead, but all of the players in the mission ahead have yet to gather. For there is a precise recipe to be followed: a journey must be taken by a very specific group.

First, a prayerful hunter must return to his home and take up his mantle as leader. With him, he must bring his bride, a daughter destined to set the kingdoms free. She will bring with her a cat transformed, able to sense the sorcery at work. Together with a warrior monk and a seeing fool, they will traverse the mountains to find the heart of what's been stolen, what's been hidden, what must be put to death.

His last word hangs in the air and I can barely breathe. What are we being called to do? How does this "gift of prophecy" work so that they knew we were coming?

"So you see, nephew, there is much ahead of you and your little group. You must not lose heart, and you must find your way to setting us free."

"You said *sorcery*." Paul looks straight at Amis and then at Jacob. "What is he speaking of?"

"Though the church claimed to have destroyed all sorcerers and those who practiced magic long ago, we now know there are small covens that have cropped up here and there. The witch who incarcerated your betrothed, for instance, was part of one. We believe these sects are working toward a larger purpose and might be aiding one of the sisters."

"Might be?"

The king clears his throat before saying, "We have no reason to think otherwise. We put a great deal of trust in the insights of our monk and loyal fool. Sorcery is poisoning us all."

"What sisters?" My mother asks.

"Excuse me?"

"You said *sisters*. What sisters?"

"Surely you know of the sisters that were bound at the end of the War of Sorcery."

"Yes. I think I met one once."

"What?" I can't help the hiss in my voice.

"I believe Ute, the sorceress bound to the mountains, was the one who taught my sister, Eufemia, who was used to carry out Ute's plans. Eufemia could spirit herself to meet with Ute in the mountains. She would then move me or herself about the kingdoms to spy out different things. There was always some insidious purpose in her dealings, something that she was about."

"I think we can assume we know that purpose." The monk steps forward. "His Majesty and I have discussed this at length. Think: what was the War of Sorcery about? Power."

My stomach twists and I look toward the door. I thought I was done with magic and anything related to it. I wanted my nightmares to simply be nightmares, my strange way of mourning for the wicked woman who acted as my guardian for most of my life.

"She wants power and a way to reunite her sisters." My mother's voice trembles.

The monk stares at her, wordless.

"Mother?" I venture.

"Though Eufemia never became a powerful sorceress like Ute, she knew a great deal and had many things she was doing to further the plans of the sisters. They were at work, always trying to find a way to reunite and undo their father's curse."

The monk's face is a scowl as he processes what she has said. The king also frowns as he speaks. "What did she have you do?"

"Like I said, I was a spy, compelled to report back on what was going on in the kingdoms where Eufemia placed me."

Jacob stares at her a little too long, his thick lips pressed firmly together. "I don't remember ever seeing you in my kingdom."

"Remember? You wouldn't recognize me. I was a cat until recently." She attempts a pitiful smile.

"What have the witches and warlocks been doing? What of Ute's plans do you know?"

"I know only that Eufemia became quite distracted in this last year by Rapunzel's small rebellion. When she did not bend to my sister's will, things began unraveling. Ute was furious with Eufemia. Plans were changing, but I never understood what. My sister reported directly to her. I only met her once myself."

The silence in the room expands, holding everyone captive. My mind is swimming as I try to understand the words my mother has spoken. This grand sorceress—Ute? —what was she planning, and why would my little rebellion cause my witch to fall out of favor?

"How does one stop a sorceress from killing kings?" My voice shocks me.

"Whoever is going to stop her must first find her," the monk replies.

The king raises one eyebrow. "Of course you must, and here we come to the crux of the matter. How will you do that?"

"You have met her?" The monk stares at my mother.

"Just once, like I said."

"Where were you?"

"A small cove in the foothills in the Soontrisse Mountains, close to King Onfroi's kingdom. But she doesn't live that close to Alleria—that's just where she trained Eufemia."

"Where does she live?"

She shakes her head, but there is a crease between her brows that causes me to wonder. "Mother?"

"She dwells in the heart."

"So close to my father's kingdom?" Paul's voice rasps.

She nods, as though she cannot bear to speak anymore.

"Then that is where we will go." The monk nods.

"Of course, and you will take them with you." The king's voice is firm; he wants no argument.

"I will gladly accompany Brother Jacob," Paul speaks up, "but there is no need for ladies to ride into certain danger."

"I say that there is. You have need of their unique insight. Amis has come to help along the way. Gather supplies—you will need to leave at first light." The Fisher King holds up a hand to dismiss us, and at once the maidservant that was attending the king is now taking away our plates. I had forgotten we were supposed to be eating. I look up at my beloved's face, still as perplexed as mine.

"How can I lead a group—this group—to stop a sorceress?" Paul stumbles through his question.

There is a silence in the air.

"Paul," Jacob says at last, "I think we should head by way of your father's kingdom. Perhaps he or your brother can help us discover more. After their loss—"

"What loss? Did something happen to Princess Aalis?"

"I'm sorry." The king clears his throat. "Of course you wouldn't know. The child—they named him Enguerrand —disappeared the winter after you went missing."

"How does an infant go missing?"

"No one knows. His mother kissed him goodnight, and the next morning he was gone. They expected a letter demanding ransom from his kidnappers, but it never came. He simply vanished into the mountains."

I reach for Paul's arm, but he pulls forward before I can touch him. "I have heard of such things, but I thought they were stories to frighten children to obey their parents."

"I wish it were not so. Your brother's wife has been inconsolable and does not receive visitors any longer, they say."

"And my brother?"

"He is well, carrying on as your father languishes. The trading between our kingdoms has continued, though I don't know how well we will fare this winter. The kingdoms that trade with us after harvest have not been doing so this year. It seems their lack of a king has caused such unrest among the commoners that some of the harvest was burned. They have barely enough for themselves and refuse to trade for fish and such. We are fortunate that some of our land has produced a crop this season, but this land is too arid to truly sustain us. Once you have helped us solve this crisis, we may have another on our hands."

Perhaps things have grown too sedate for our jester. He claps his hands all at once and flips about the room. "We need to make plans to move. Come now, one crisis at a time is all that Amis can afford!"

The king gives a hollow chuckle. "The strange times you have ahead of you! I wish I could come."

"If you could come, we would not need to go." Amis claps again, but none of us can laugh.

THE HANDFASTING

The king begins insisting on several things before we leave his chambers. I am taken aback when Jacob speaks up. "Your intentions, Your Majesty, are well and good, but you have never been on a quest of this sort before."

"Neither have you!" The king parries with his wry smile.

"No, but I have journeyed into the unknown before. We must pack light, travel quickly, and above all, be united in our purpose. Though I do not relish the thought of taking two women with me—" he sends a glance our way "—I understand that it is necessary to bring them along. I know that Paul will be a help, but he and Rapunzel must not travel unmarried. As Amis prophesied, she must be his bride."

I start at this.

"I see what you mean," murmurs the king.

I object. "I don't. We were traveling just fine from Rona."

"You had separate sleeping quarters. As we travel

through mountains, you will need the protection of a husband," Jacob insists.

"And my mother?"

"She will have the protection of the son your marriage will provide her, and I will do my best by her."

"And I!" Amis flips to emphasize his enthusiasm.

But Brother Jacob ignores him, his large, dark eyes piercing. "The handfasting must be done tonight, and supplies must be gathered so that we can leave in the morning. I am sorry for the rush, but now that we are all together, we must proceed. I believe the hand of God has brought us together. We must begin our journey at once."

"Before we have met with Paul's family?" I cannot stop the quiver that makes my voice tremble.

Paul takes my hand. "I told you before, my dear—my father does not mind who I marry unless my uncle does."

Despite Paul's attempt to mollify me, my mind is a-whirl. How can I become part of a family without knowing the people in it? I don't even understand what it means to be in a family except for the short time I spent traveling with Edmund's mother, sharing her gentle wisdom and kind heart. Surely, it is foolish to marry a girl without your father and mother knowing and approving.

"There can be no delay, then." The king is quick to agree with Brother Jacob. "Will you perform the hand-fasting before you set off?"

"It is usually done at dawn, but I think this time we should perform it at sunset when both the moon and the sun are present in the sky."

"If you think it best."

The monk looks over at Paul. "We should give the couple that much before rushing into danger." He attempts what I think is supposed to be a smile.

Without further discussion, we are pushed out of the

king's presence so that my mother and I can ready ourselves for the evening's handfasting. We haven't much time, but I am glad that I am already wearing my favorite green gowns despite getting dressed in the dark this morning. A maid comes to help us with our hair and I sit in silence, though my mind is spinning.

⌒⊙⟡⊙⌒

It is nearing sunset and I am standing in the gardens of the king. The air is cooling, and the flowering rosebushes nearby tell me that autumn is approaching. No longer dressed in warrior's garb, Brother Jacob is arrayed in a black satin robe embroidered with gold crosses. He stands before us and makes the sign of the cross after Paul and I kneel before him. In Latin, he blesses us and prays for God to be glorified in our union. He then asks us simple questions about our roles in marriage. Will we honor and forsake all others for the privilege of uniting together? My voice trembles when I agree to do so. Paul's hoarse answer makes my eyes tear with gratitude. The monk takes his white satin sash and wraps our hands together, and I realize that I am now bound to this man forever. For a moment I can't breathe. Do we know one another well enough to do right by each other on this journey? How will we fight the dark magic ahead?

I am overwhelmed as we walk into the Great Hall afterwards. Brother Jacob cautions us to drink lightly, but eat well. The hall is filled with all sorts of people, loud and clamoring, happy that we have wed, even though they don't know me.

The evening is a haze of well-greetings by the common people who toast our good health. I take tiny sips, as the line is long, the dry red wine is strong, and I do not wish to get drunk. I have never done so before, but I've seen many who have—and I have never enjoyed their antics or loss of decorum. There is dancing, and I remember that night not so long ago when I rediscovered Paul in a different Great Hall, placed there by the witch with his memories of me erased. Oh, how I cried when I realized that he was alive but that I couldn't be with him!

The witch did so much to hurt me; I feel bitterness try to take over my heart at the memory. I fight it down, determined to not become like her—bitter and incapable of forgiving. I chose to forgive her; surely I can cling to that when I now know that Paul has been set free from her wickedness and we will live as one.

My eyes flick towards my mother, sitting alone, unsettled, though she tries to smile when she sees I am looking at her. I am glad she is coming with us. I am certain I need her by my side, to help me understand who I am and how to become who I want to be.

Am I thinking too much? Paul lifts me from the ground with a great flourish, my skirts twirling out around me as he spins me around. Yes, tonight is a good night. I will think more about the danger and the fear tomorrow. I will focus on the man who longs to hold me.

◌⁂◌

I WAKE, and bit by bit I am conscious of something. My mind is slow to recognize that there is someone else near me. I hear Paul breathing. Turning on my side I light the candle, hoping that my movements won't wake him. I want to look at my beloved, to treasure the sight of him resting by my side. I want to remember this moment of calm rest before whatever it is we are about to head into. My heart squeezes at the thought of what is ahead. Everything I have experienced since leaving my tower warns me that there is more to come. I push the thoughts backward, as though there is a way to make them disappear if I shove hard enough.

Paul's chest rises and falls in gentle rhythm and he turns to me in sleep. Without opening his eyes, a smile curls the edges of his lips. All at once he grabs me and pulls me tightly to his chest. I give a strange little squeal of delight.

"What was that?" he laughs.

I feel my face warm as he stares into my eyes and then his look lingers on my lips. "I don't know . . . I guess I'm just happy."

"I like when you're happy."

The grin that covers my face feels absurd, but I can't stop it. With Paul I am childlike, free, innocent. His love covers me and I feel cherished, wrapped up in invisible armor—but will it keep me safe from all that we may encounter?

Paul pulls back to look at me. "Is something wrong?" he asks.

"No, of course not."

"Rapunzel?"

"I'm so happy right now, in this moment—I don't want to leave this room. I don't know what we are about to do, where we will go and what will we see? What does this sorceress want, what does she—"

His hand gently covers my lips. "Perhaps we should ask God to cover our fears."

I know that Paul trusts absolutely in God. He would not go on this quest if he did not believe in the deepest parts of his soul that this is what God desires for him. I should have known that he would want to share this faith with me, that he would want me to trust as well.

"I don't know how to do that. I don't know that I *can*

do that." I think of how I had just started trusting in God when Edmund used his power to take control of me. Why didn't God save me from that pain? As much as I don't want to think of it, I feel anger at Edmund's abuse. The doubt in me spreads like an inky darkness, tainting what was joyful only moments before.

Paul doesn't see my struggle; he has already closed his hazel eyes. He takes a deep breath. "God of heaven and earth, we are afraid, but I believe you are sending us out. Protect us from the evil one, give us victory to free this land from those who would hurt your leaders." His eyes open.

"Is that all?"

"That is all, Rapunzel. Faith isn't a complicated thing, it is simple. I prayed to find you, remember? When I couldn't find my way to the mist that led me back to you, I closed my eyes and prayed. God is greater than magic."

I look away from him. I'm not certain he's right, but I am glad that he has his faith. What must it be like to trust? "Is it easy?"

"I said it was simple, not easy."

I don't really understand what he means by that, but I nod and his lips find mine once more. The knock on the bedchamber's door brings our kisses to a halt.

Paul is quick to dress and closes the curtains around our bed before he opens the door. I hear his voice as he answers my mother. "Yes?"

"I'm sorry, Paul, but we must be getting ready. Brother Jacob says there is no time to linger. Is our girl—" But I come out from behind the curtains knowing she has seen me in my chemise before. "I'm here."

"Good, let's go get you ready. They have already selected our horses for the trip."

I laugh at the look on her face. "Mother, have you never ridden before?" I shouldn't laugh, not really, since it was only recently that I learned how to ride and I haven't had as much practice as I would like before beginning such a journey.

"I did, long ago, but I have not ridden since being Cat."

"Well," says Paul, smirking, "this should make for an interesting journey. I have never seen a cat mount a horse before."

"Can't we just walk?"

"There are times we will have to." Paul nods, his brow drawn now. "But we must move with urgency. I agree with Brother Jacob, time is essential to our well-being. The kings must not be allowed to suffer longer than necessary, and we must race against winter to get to the heart before Ute has her way. You ladies will have to ride."

"Perhaps it will all come back to me." My mother gives a shrug of one shoulder.

RIDING AWAY

I stare down at the riding clothes. "I can't wear this! It's not proper!"

Paul laughs as he comes back to check on my mother and me. "Rapunzel, you've never ridden astride, but for this trip, you will need to."

"But the—the skirt—!" I am at a loss to describe how indecent I feel showing off my legs. The sideless surcoat covers the cotehardie, but the cotehardie itself is slit on the sides all the way up to my hips and seems an indecent length.

"—is short, I know, but it will make it easier when we hike, and the slits will make it easier for you to mount and maintain your seat."

"But people will see my legs like this!"

My mother is now behind the dressing screen, putting on a similar outfit.

"Which is why you are wearing hosen beneath. Believe me, you'll be thankful for the extra material." Paul is amused by my distress.

The dark blue wool is soft and must have been shorn

from a lamb. I am glad for its texture, but—I take a deep breath. My mother comes out from behind the screen looking uncomfortable as well.

She looks at my appalled expression and tilts her head, mischievously lifting a corner of her skirts. We both giggle.

Paul rolls his eyes at us, but laughs. "The court cobbler worked all night on these." He gestures to the brown leather boots that will lace up to our thighs. I've never worn anything like them. My feet are used to my soft, pointed shoes that have often had to be replaced during my travels. Having a hard sole feels unnatural to me, but Paul assures me that I will be thankful as the trip wears on.

The king is not well enough to see us off, but Paul says a quick goodbye before we head out. The dawn has begun to light the sky when we mount our horses in the inner bailey. I am surprised to see that my mother needs minimal assistance in mounting while I take my time with Paul's help. My horse is a mare like Paul's, though she is honey-colored, short, and muscular. They say this breed was specifically bred for climbing into the mountains. Paul has a long relationship with this kind of horse, having grown up in his father's mountain kingdom. I am unsure of how the climbing will affect our ride, though I know it will slow things down. The ideas of heights and horses and balancing astride all combine to make a knot in my stomach. I will master this, though.

I was once terrified of horses, but I had Gwynndolen's help to overcome it. The daughter of a lord I visited while betrothed to Edmund in the summer, she offered her help and friendship without guile. I now think how proud she would be of me as I set off on this little adventure. It makes me sad to think I will likely never see her again; I felt a kinship to her that I have had with only a few others. Why have I never been able to keep close to me those that

I love? Over the past year, I made my first friends . . . and I lost every one of them.

I suppose this includes Paul, though I have him back now. Perhaps that bodes well for future relationships.

I realize with a shock of regret that I even miss Edmund. We were friends before he began controlling me. I miss that friendship before it became the distorted, mangled thing it was before we parted. Should I feel disloyal thinking such thoughts? I am a married woman now—does that mean I must not think of other men? I look at my mother, thinking she might know how to advise me. Sometimes it's as though she can hear what I'm thinking, but not now. She is leaning forward over her horse, stroking its neck and speaking softly. This reminds me of how Gwynndolen first encouraged me to bond with her mare, and so I do so, too.

Dressed in chain mail like Paul and Jacob, Amis comes out into the inner bailey carrying several bags. "So we are off, are we?"

Both men go over to help secure the bags on the pack horses. "Yes."

"The ladies look ready for anything. I hope we all are."

Jacob shakes his head. "I will lead us in prayer before we head out." His prayer is sedate and colorless compared to what Paul prayed this morning.

As we leave the castle and head through the market town outside the portcullis, I notice the people milling around. My mother laughs, but I'm not sure why. Sometimes she makes little sounds that make me think her mind is addled after all of her years of being feline. Cats think themselves superior to us; perhaps she still feels that way. If I'm honest, I sometimes feel that way myself, though I spend an equal amount of time feeling substandard to those around me.

Everyone seems to know what is expected of them, how to act, how to communicate. Though it is not as bad as when I first left my tower, still people look at me oddly, and I know that I'm not always reacting or responding as expected. Is that a bad thing? Perhaps it is not. Surely people need a little jolt of an oddity in their lives. I wonder, if God did make me then his plan must be for my peculiarity to change the perspective of those around me.

I wish he had not. What would I have been like if I had grown up without the witch? Most people grow up with a father and mother in a village with brothers and sisters and friends. If God is as powerful as I've been told, why did he allow the sorceress and the witch power to do evil? I fear I will never understand these questions that float around my head.

My eyes snap shut as though to turn my thoughts away from these frustrations. When I open them, I stare in awe at the mountains. They are lovely! Directly ahead are foothills that are covered in green and gold foliage. There is a grey space where Paul says there is a pass between cliffs. Above that the mountains are smokey purple. The very tips of the peaks are already white with snow.

I could see them from the ship, but now I feel a tremor pulse through me. Somewhere in those mountains is the power that is poisoning the kings of these lands. A thought occurs to me. When will this poison hurt my beloved? He is the heir. What if the king dies before we are able to undo this wretched curse upon the land? Will Paul be next? If only we could understand now before going any further what it is that the sorceress is really doing. How is weakening the kings going to make way for her to be reunited with her sisters? Why would a dejected kingdom make the world ripe for sorcery?

The mare beneath me follows Paul's lead as we

continue, and I hold the reins with a gentle grip as I've been taught. The road before us is no longer white, but a dusty brown. Grasslands stretch out in a fallow field to the right. Beyond that I see that the farmland has shared its harvest and is now awaiting winter. We are following the Ventrias River that will lead us up into the mountains. Its source rests in King Onfroi's kingdom, where there are hot springs said to have healing powers. What good are those healing powers if the king is lying sick in bed, unable to govern or care for his people?

My mind drifts back over my travels. I think of kind Dorothea tucked into the heart of the Deep Wood. She cared for any who came near her door, believing she was there to do the work of "the God of heaven," as she called him. She helped me to see that I couldn't keep living my life looking backward. She said she wasn't using magic, but there were things she told me about that defied the natural order of life. I feel my forehead crease in confusion. If the God of heaven truly doesn't care for magic in his followers, why does he use it? Or is he magic himself and he will not be used?

I know that Dorothea loved him, and he guided people to her so that she could help them, but is that magic or just awe-inspiring power? I had almost made up my mind to follow God, but now . . . I remember the map in the Great Hall; the source of the Auriel which waters the Deep Wood is also in the Soontrisse Mountains and flows into the hill country near the convent where I stayed last year for a time. If I understood how to pray, I would pray for these friends that I left behind. Surely this God of heaven loves them if he truly is their creator. Can't he save us all from this torment and Ute's temper tantrum?

THE PAST COMES NEAR

*I*t is getting near evening when we come to a small inn. The mountains loom larger than ever in the distance. I smile as Paul helps me down from my mount. Oh, it feels good to have ground beneath my feet again!

The inn is small, but there are enough rooms that we can stay the night. Paul and I will not be together like we were last night as the men and women bed in separate rooms. I can't help sighing since I was looking forward to resting in his arms again.

The floor is dirty, carpeted by moldy rushes and scraps of food the tall dog hasn't licked up yet. One of the daughters of the inn brings us little fish pies that are crisp but tasteless, lacking their customary sweet-and-sour tang. The ale she pours *is* sour, and I grimace after she leaves us.

The room gives off a rank odor when we enter, and my mother laughs when I decide to sleep against the wall rather than lie on the floor's bedding. "I would think that with all your travel—"

"Traveling doesn't mean one has to settle for something filthy. I would rather sleep outside than in here."

"I understand. Being outside is a great comfort to you after being within that tower for so long."

I look at her as the light from our single candle wavers across her face, so like my own—but there is so much she keeps from me. "What was my father like? I don't even know his name." Why does my voice sound accusing? My mother looks up at me with hurt across her features. "I'm sorry, but I know almost nothing about what life I could have had with you if only—"

"If only I had not been so greedy?" Her smile is sad and I feel a pang of guilt. Still, I want to know, I need to know. She picks at her bedding and finally settles against the wall next to me with a sigh. I am glad there are no other travelers to share the room with so we can have privacy. "Your father was a good man. He had hair like yours, though shorter and even curlier. When the sun would shine down into the foothills where we lived, his hair would glint and glitter. I loved teasing him about it when we were children."

"You grew up together?"

"Of course. We lived in the same village. That is the way it usually is, Rapunzel."

I feel stupid and small—how should I know such things? She must see the look of pain on my face because her low tone softens and she reaches to hold my hand. "Your father was kind, much kinder than I was. I longed for him to notice me, but I was so young and, you see, Eufemia was a year older than I. Oh, Rapunzel, she was so beautiful with her black hair and flawless white skin. She had a graceful way of standing, just like our mother. Her eyes were green."

"Like mine?"

"Like ours. Green eyes are not so common, have you noticed? But the women in our family all have them. When I first saw you, I thought how your father would love your eyes."

"But you were a cat then."

"I was changed into one after I gave birth to you. I thought that one day Eufemia would give us back to one another. She would remember how to forgive, how we used to be friends . . . That was while you were very young. I gave up hoping after a while.

"Did you know she would often torment me with a glimpse of you? No matter where I was, I might suddenly see a vision of you. When you first began to crawl, to walk. Sometimes she would make the visions last, and I could see the garden where you grew up. It was the garden where I decided to betray her. You would be playing together and laughing." My mother looks down, but not before I see tears fill her eyes. "She made certain I knew when she killed him—your father. I never thought she could do such a thing. We had been such friends when we were young . . ."

"What happened? What drove you apart?"

"She loved your father, Guarin, but he loved me. Perhaps he could have grown to love her, but she became strange as we grew older."

"The witch"—I can never seem to call her my *aunt* —"told me she was cursed as a child and that it made her strange. Did everyone hate her because of it?"

"People did look at her strangely. Something twisted inside her when that old woman cursed her, and she began running off every chance she could. Though we had always been together and loved to play, something in her stopped loving anyone but herself then. How can I explain this . . .? It was as though she was consumed, like something had taken hold of her. She was never the same. When we got a little older, she became an apprentice to a widow up in the cove, or so we thought."

"Who was she really with?" I ask, but I know the answer and my stomach turns. I wish I hadn't eaten.

"Ute, the sorceress. She shape-shifted to make my mother, your grandmother, think that she was the Widow Osterhild. But all along it was Ute, giving Eufemia lessons in sorcery."

I shake my head. "How could your mother not know? And what of your father? Parents are supposed to protect their children." How could parents have a child and not know what that child was doing? If you love someone young and vulnerable, wouldn't you keep watch over them? Parents should keep them safe at home!

I don't know what my face looks like, but my mother begins to laugh as she blinks back tears. "Oh, Rapunzel, they couldn't watch us every moment of the day! You know what it is like to be locked up—would you want anyone else to suffer from a 'love' like that? Besides, Eufemia was a great hand with the needle, and my parents honestly believed she was an apprentice. She was supposed to be learning how to weave cloth. The widow had an amazing loom her husband had once built her. All the families around, even the king over the mountain, had become dependent on her little enterprise. It made sense for Euphemia to go and learn from her.

"She would come back to town with the work we thought she and the old woman had made together. If only you could have seen the change that came over her. Eufemia was sullen and cross most of the time. Whenever I asked why she was like that, my mother said it was because she was becoming a woman. I remember my father saying that he wished he had had sons."

I frown at that and my mother laughs again.

"Your grandfather was not a nice man, but we should also remember that girls can be very difficult at that age, Rapunzel. I know I was, even when I was helping. My mother had me at work in the home and around our small goat farm making cheese. I took the milk to town every day, and there I would see your father. Oh, my heart ached for the love of him, but I knew that Eufemia wanted him, too.

"I'm not sure how Eufemia thought she would capture Guarin's heart. She no longer saw him in town. She no longer went to Mass. It wasn't long after she left that he began courting me and we wed. You know, I went to visit once—to show her how happy I was. I, the untalented sister, had found a husband. But when I got to the cove, I saw Ute for myself."

I am disturbed by the silence that invades the room. Evil feels tangible, present, but I have to know. "What was she like?"

"Terrifying. A great dragon with shining purple scales —and when she became a woman, her voice was hard, frigid. She warned me away. I never went back." She looks at me with regret. "I wish I had. That winter was hard, but then, Eufemia took her earnings and bought a house. This was unheard of! A young maid not marrying, but instead buying her own house? It was scandalous. But the family she bought from was only too glad to take the money and cared nothing for convention or the proper order of things." My mother's eyes have filmed over with the painful memory, gaze far removed from the dim room. Her pupils are large and I can barely see her green irises.

"Perhaps it would have been fine for her to live on her own. I suppose many women can live without a husband, but at the time I thought everyone's life needed to look the same. I thought she was trying to hurt us by being different."

She takes a deep breath. "When she moved into town, I spied a beautiful bright purple-leafed plant in her garden. She knew how fond I was of lettuce. Something came over me—it might have been because I was pregnant with you. I couldn't help myself, I begged her for more and more. After awhile she made excuses and denied me. It was easy to send your father to get some for me. You see, I needed that plant, Rapunzel. I had dreams that if I did not eat it, you would die within me."

I think of my friend Adeliza and the horrible night she lost her baby. "Had you lost a child?"

"Yes, right after I was married, and I was convinced I would again." My mother's voice grates on me as she justifies her actions. "The nightmares came every night. Your father kept bringing the plant home, but he was downcast and I knew I shouldn't ask him to do it. I couldn't stop—at least, I didn't make myself. He should have said *no*, but he didn't. You know what happened."

She had allowed me to be traded for the plant. Her greed had sold me. Did it matter that the witch had found a way to entice her, to manipulate her?

"Eufemia knew when the birth pangs were coming. She arrived as I was struggling to have you. At first I was glad she was there, but then I learned your father had traded you for the lettuce. For lettuce, Rapunzel. All because of my greed. When you came into the world, she transformed me into Cat. I never even got to hold you. I only stayed with your father for a short time while I healed from the birthing. The witch had work for me to do." She pulls my hand to her heart. "Rapunzel, I can never tell you how sorry I am for what I did, for how I treated my sister and how that hurt—"

I jerk away so I won't hear any more. Everything feels tangled up inside me; I want to scream at the injustice of my life. If I forgave my mother and the witch, then why does my chest feel frozen? It's hard to breathe. For a long moment, I stare at her. "We should get some rest."

Her hand is against her chest as though I've struck her. I blow out the candle and leave her in the dark.

A FOOL

The next morning we have runny porridge, which is preferable to the dried provisions we will be eating on our journey when we make camp along the way. The sour ale has not improved a bit, and I hope that other inns will be better than this.

I don't know what to say to my mother after her confessional from the night before. Did she really tell me anything I hadn't already suspected? No, but hearing it, knowing what a good life she had once had, hurt me. It could have been our good life, if only—

My stomach twists as a tally of wrongs begins to count off in my head. I know I have made mistakes and have chosen to do things I should not. Last spring and summer, I went with Edmund, allowed him to control me. Ignorance kept me from realizing I could choose for myself— but still, I gave part of myself away—betrayed myself. What I did worked alongside the plans the witch had for me and extended her power over me. In my journeys over the past year, I left behind friend after friend. That feels wrong—friends are made to stand together throughout time. If I am not free of guilt, then who am I to condemn my mother?

But the truth is, I do. There is a hard stone toward her where my warm heart should be.

I smile at my husband and banish thoughts of our many wrongs. I won't wish I had left her behind. We need each other—she is part of this, and I need her. If I cannot forgive her out of good will, I will make myself do it. I will choose to live the way that I should, and we will continue this journey. We must, if we are to relieve the kingdom of this curse.

⁂

BEFORE SETTING OFF, Jacob says the morning prayer and then addresses us, though he is looking intently at Paul. "As you know, there are a few trails that lead into the mountains, and we must decide now which one we want to use. You know the horses are the best in the kingdom. They can handle the steepest trail that runs beside the Ventrias, which is the fastest way to the top. I know you said you would prefer, however, to take the slower, longer route. Perhaps we can push the horses and ourselves hard enough that we can reach the top in a good amount of time—but I must say that I have been watching the sky, and I believe that this season will not be kind to us."

Amis shrugs. "You are saying that no matter which way we go, it will be difficult."

The monk nods and leans his head forward. "It is a mountain we are heading into, as well as bad weather."

Everyone looks at Paul. He gives a little laugh, but it does not sound confident. "I think we will have to—" He turns to me, his eyes searching for an answer. I am bewildered by his expression. He seems so unlike himself. "We will go the short route. The horses will do well and keep us safe." He keeps looking at me, not at Jacob. "I am sorry. I wish I could make it easier on you."

I try to laugh, but I feel unnerved by his caution. "You said it was simple, not easy."

Though they haven't made me feel any better, my words seem to calm him a bit and he takes a deep breath.

Paul helps me up into my saddle, which is good since I am so stiff. "Ladies, I know that you are sore this morning, and you will grow more so until your bodies acclimate to riding. For the horses' sakes as well as yours, we should probably walk a little today. I have learned that some walking coupled with a good bit of riding makes for a better journey."

I look ahead and think of walking into the hills—and beyond that, into the mountains. I take a deep breath. We can do this.

⚬⚬⚬⚬

PAUL MOUNTS his horse and gives an uncertain look back at Jacob, who nods him on. Paul tries to smile and takes the lead. There is no room for our horses to walk side by side, so we line up: me following Paul, then next my mother, followed by Jacob who leads a pack horse, and after that Amis bringing up the rear with another pack horse.

The land swells upward as we venture into the foothills. The trail, which was already narrow, thins, and the horses group together even more closely. I'm surprised—I would have thought they would want some room between heads and tails, but they seem happy to be near one another.

We are right next to the river now, and the sound of the rushing water is soothing. The trees multiply all around us, and birds flit to and fro. They are louder than the water! I feel myself relax after the initial tension. I adjust my seating now that I know how my mare's gait changes as she travels up the incline. The sounds surrounding me lighten my thoughts, and I laugh at the antics of a couple of squirrels. The cool breeze brushes against my face as the humidity of the sea slowly drops away. If the rest of the trip is like this, we will get along very well, my mare and me.

Paul turns in his seat to look back at us. "Have we ridden far enough, ladies? What do you say to walking till midday?"

I try to swing my leg over the back of the saddle, but my leg no longer listens to me. I drag myself off and stumble into Paul's arms. My body aches in parts that I have never thought about before. I haven't felt sore like this since I stopped traveling on foot.

My mare nudges me with her nose, so I pull an apple out of the knapsack I got at the inn. I have begun thinking of my mare as "Honey," and I like that. My spirits lift a bit even as I try not to groan in pain. I walk to the side of my horse, trying to adjust to the pinch of the hard boots that won't let me feel the terrain. I wonder what it will be like as we get higher and higher. The time passes quickly, and I feel embarrassed when Paul turns to look at me when my stomach rumbles. I didn't know it was loud enough for others to hear!

"We are coming to a clearing—and I think Rapunzel is ready to stop."

We break for a rest, water the horses downstream, and replenish the water bladders. My feet beg me to free them for a quick soak, but I doubt I'll get them back into the boots if I do. A quick glance over at Jacob reveals he must be deep in thought, though his eyes dart at every little sound. I get the feeling that this monk is constantly praying and always alert to what is going on around him.

A sigh gushes out as I sit down, and Amis laughs. "You sound like I feel!"

"But you've ridden before."

"Not too many hills in Maer."

"How long were you there serving as jester?"

Everyone is listening as we hand around our dried provisions and drink from the bladder of watered wine Jacob says will help with the aches. My mother keeps casting side-glances my way, and I make myself smile at her.

Amis settles into his tale with a smile. He has no energy for flips or singing, but his voice still carries the excitement of a true storyteller. "I served with my father, who chose to travel whenever he grew tired of a lord or king."

"But how do you get leave to do such a thing?"

"Father was not a man to ask for leave, he simply left. Mother died when I was very young." He chews, his thick eyebrows pulled down. "I don't remember her face, just her voice. It was lovely, and she would sing with my father sometimes. After she died, here in the Northlands, my father got itchy feet. He had enough talent that he was welcomed wherever he went, but he also made some enemies by not settling down. I spent most of my time in Maer, but when I met you, Lady Rapunzel, I could no longer forget my dreams. It was time to return to the land of my birth."

"But how did you know that I would be here?"

"I told you before, I could not forget my dreams. You understand, don't you?"

I start to nod when my mother sits forward. "So you dream of things that come to pass? Some might call that sorcery."

Jacob frowns. "It is only sorcery when the supernatural is manipulated by man outside of God's will. The king and I believe this is a gift of prophecy, a message from God."

My mother cocks her head and looks long at Jacob without blinking, as though he is a puzzle she would like to solve. He doesn't seem disturbed, and I notice a hint of a smile around his lips as he meets her gaze. At last she sits back. "I suppose that could be true."

Amis lifts his brows and his eyes widen. "But would God choose to use a fool?"

"He spoke out of a donkey's mouth, why not a fool?" Paul laughs and we all join in, though I must remember to ask later about the story of a speaking donkey.

We ride and walk and ride again. At last we find our way into a small town as darkness begins covering us like a blanket. Once the horses have been watered and brushed down, we hobble them because there is no place to board them. We make our way to a family home that is open to travelers and enjoy a hearty vegetable stew for supper. The ale here has a foamy head that coats my upper lip. I wipe it away with a smile and reach for the fresh bread the alewife has brought.

We eat outside under the trees, overlooking the river. "During winter, the current keeps the river moving so swiftly that it never freezes over." Paul says with a smile. I love to see the creases in the laugh lines around his eyes.

"Did you ever winter in Trisse?" I wonder aloud.

"Once. My uncle's wife was to have a child just a few years ago. Some thought I would be upset, since he would be heir, but I wasn't. I wanted the child to grow to be a great man, but he was stillborn and my aunt died. That winter was horrid, and my mother and I stayed on to help my uncle through the loss."

"I am sorry." My fingers touch the sleeve of his arm.

He now wears the royal blue of the Fisher King under his chain mail. The blue suits him and makes me think of the waters he will rule one day. Surely this man has many untold stories, many things I don't know about. What if he would have preferred a quiet life outside of court and rulings? Could he have been happy as a simple hunter and not have to worry about the administration of a large kingdom, not have to chase after a bewitched girl, not have to track down a sorceress? He is a quiet man who enjoys a good story, a great hunt—

What if my life were not entwined with his? Would he be happier? I frown; it is too late to think such thoughts. We have been married less than a week and here I am, worried it was all a mistake and I will pull him down into my vortex. What kind of wife will I be if I continue in this fashion? I wish I could ask my mother, but I cannot. What kind of wife was she, sending out her husband to go and steal? What kind of wife will I be, coming from such a woman?

I must stop these thoughts! We go sleep inside the single cramped room the family shares. I snuggle my back into Paul as he pulls me close beneath a coarse blanket.

THE HELPMEET

After another day of riding and walking, the men gather firewood while my mother and I gather apples. I sit beside Paul when we come together to eat, and Jacob smiles at us.

"Rapunzel, I hear you have very little training in the ways of our God."

I feel the heat on my face, and it isn't from the orange flames. "It is true that my guardian—"

"The witch? Ute's pupil?"

"Yes, she hated God."

"Did she teach you to hate him?"

"I suppose she tried. She showed me how flawed his people were and that he could not be trusted."

He says nothing to interrupt me, just nods. I feel Paul's gaze on me and I wonder what he is thinking. What will he do if Jacob disapproves of me? Is it too late for such things? We are married, after all, and by the man who is watching me, judging me.

"Do you know that man was made first, and then woman?"

This was not what I thought he would say. "I did not know that."

He chews the apple my mother has handed him and nods before swallowing. "Yes, you see, God made the world out of nothing. He called light out of darkness, separated the land and the waters, made plants and creatures—and last, he made man. But man was alone, and God saw that, though everything else in creation was good, this was not good. So, after the first man looked throughout the animal kingdom for a proper mate, he was exhausted. God caused a deep sleep to fall on the man. As he slept, God took a rib from the side of the man and created a woman, a help-meet for the man. Can you imagine that? God knew man would need a partner in life, someone beside him."

I can't help but smile. Does this mean I have a purpose, that I can be of use to Paul? Perhaps I *can* be of help, even though Paul thought at first to leave me behind. Somehow this life together will be wonderful. My fingers intertwine with his, but then a question comes to mind. "But what of you? Aren't you alone?"

Jacob nods, his walnut-brown face somber. "That's as it should be. Priests are monks who have a special gift and calling that keeps us committed to God alone. We are not distracted by a wife or children."

The momentary lift falters. Am I a distraction for Paul? I think of the Fisher King and all Paul said he was able to do in the last several years, the many improvements Paul related he had made to the castle, the way his people appreciated his whole-hearted devotion. Was his wife a distraction, and once she was gone, he became a better king? I wish I did not think such things, even if they might be true. Once I have thought them, it seems that they are true, they are real.

I take a deep breath and determine within myself not

to be an albatross. I will be a—what did Jacob call wives? A *helpmeet.* I will help Paul. We won't have to go slower. I won't complain anymore, no matter how sore my blistered feet get. He will be glad to have me along. If one day this creator-god does bless us with children, then we will have a great many stories to tell them. There will be many things to say of our first adventure in marriage.

As we eat in companionable quiet, I try to picture myself as a mother. It is not as hard as I would have supposed. I will cuddle and kiss and sing. My mind envisions being able to stay by their bedside at night and hold their sweet little hands during the day. It will be my duty and pleasure to serve them, not to leave them as some parents do. I will not allow them to wander free without guidance.

I glance at my poor mother. Even if she does say that my grandparents meant well, their protection was weak, their guidance was lacking. We will do better than that—not oppressive like my witch or neglectful like my grandparents. I—*we* will find the balance, and our children—princes and princesses!—will know such love and devotion.

These happy thoughts chatter in my mind as we prepare for bed. When Paul wraps his arms around me, I turn to him and ask, "How many children do you want?"

He laughs. "As many as the Lord will give us. Why? How many do you want?"

"Do you think that ten is too many?"

"Ten!"

"Yes, ten sounds a good, round number. We will not be lacking for anything, and I was once in the home of a family with ever so many children running about. They were happy even though they only had one great family room and they shared it with animals."

"That is the way of most peasants."

"I would be a peasant if not for you."

"I would be happy to be a peasant with you." He leans close and kisses my neck.

"What would you do? What would you be if you could not be a king?"

He takes only a moment. "I would do what I like best —I would hunt."

I laugh out loud before thinking of the others nearby who can hear. Lowering my voice, I say, "I wish you could hunt now. Would you take me with you?"

"On a hunt?"

"Gwynndolen told me—"

"Who?"

"Gwynndolen, she was the daughter of a lord in Rona when I was traveling—" but I don't finish the thought.

"With Edmund."

"Yes." I swallow hard. Why does he sound like that? "Gwynndolen was the one who taught me how to ride sidesaddle."

Paul is nodding. I can see his outline by the light of the moon filtering through the trees overhead. He seems like he wants to say something, but he is silent.

"Gwynndolen said that nobles liked to go out for a hunt on horses. That was why she taught me to ride, though we didn't go for a hunt. Her father wasn't well, you see."

It remains quiet for so long that I wonder if he has fallen asleep. His breathing is regular, so I startle when he finally does speak. "I would rather not speak of the time you spent on Rona."

I can't let that pass. "I thought you were dead, Paul."

"I know."

"And you had forgotten me, forgotten your whole life."

"I know. But now we are together and I would rather not be reminded of our separation—or of him."

"Paul, you need to know something. Please—" I can feel him withdrawing. "Listen, I never loved Edmund, not even for a moment. I loved you."

He is still, I can barely hear him breathe. "Then why did you stay with him?"

"I was weak and confused, and I didn't understand my feelings for him. I found him attractive, but there were things about him I couldn't trust."

"But you trust me?"

"Of course I do."

He goes quiet again, and I wrap myself tighter to him. It's cold, but I would need to be closer even if it were hot. "Please don't pull away. You scare me when you do." I wonder whether it is wise to say this aloud. I don't know if a man and wife should discuss such things, but I can only guess how things should be between us. It occurs to me that perhaps Paul is as confused as I am about what a husband and wife should act like with one another. "I know I'm not like your mother."

"What?"

"I mean, I'm not like the queen you want me to be."

He sighs and at last holds me close again. "Rapunzel, you are exactly who I want you to be."

I shake my head. I'm not really saying this the right way, but I don't know how to untangle my words. They keep getting snarled, leaving me unsure of what I want to say to him right now. The fatigue from the day is setting into my speech, clouding my thoughts and thickening my tongue. "I don't want you to be angry with me."

"I'm not."

"I have wanted to be with you and only you since we first met."

"I know."

"You do?"

"I do."

This should bring me peace, but it doesn't. I lean forward and kiss him, and he kisses me back, but it is a shallow kiss and he turns to lay on his back. I rest my head on his chest and slowly allow sleep to claim me as I listen to his heartbeat.

THE SWAN AND THE DRAGON

The next day is more of the same. We are deep in the foothills and the leaves are no longer just green and golden—there are some turning scarlet and sunset orange, a few falling to the ground to be crunched under foot and hoof. Overhead I hear the honks of geese flying south. I wrap myself tighter in the hooded cloak that warms my body.

When we come to the fire in the evening, Amis surprises us with a little show. He juggles four apples and then tries to get us to juggle them with him. I am awful at this and can't seem to keep them moving at the right speed. Paul is, not surprisingly, well-coordinated. We clap and laugh at his new talent. I snuggle close to my beloved and listen to the fire crackle when the flames feast on the bit of moisture hidden in the wood.

Amis waggles his eyebrows, as he loves to do, and begins his tale, again without singing it. He tells us that riding in the mountain air makes it hard to sing, but he can't resist telling a tale around a fire, even if the fire makes him hoarse.

"There were two daughters once, and their father was a king. I suppose that means they were princesses. Against the custom, the younger was to wed before the elder. Unusual," he says to the surprised look on my mother's face, "but I think you know something of this yourself, do you not?" He gives a little chuckle and I look to see how my mother receives this gentle teasing. She tenses and looks away. "The elder wanted to marry, but her betrothed had died that year in the War of Sorcery. When the sisters were walking by the river one day, the elder pushed the younger into the rushing waters. She screamed, begging her sister to save her. But the elder said she would only help if the younger gave up her betrothed to the elder."

My mother snorts. "What sort of man would allow himself to be passed around among sisters?"

"What sort indeed? Not the sort that sits here around this fire." His voice is merry and his dark eyes twinkle, as though the tale he is weaving is a happy sort, instead of the kind that trips over the wounds of my family. "The younger was pulled quickly into the current of the river. She was able to swim for a time, but at last she could no longer surface for air. Down, down into the waters she went, and deep below she traveled. She popped up when she came to a miller's dam, her golden hair streaming around her, her red cloak looking like blood on a mirror.

"The miller's daughter saw her and fished her out with the help of her brother. When they pulled her out at last, the younger sister was no longer a princess. She had transformed into a beautiful, though dead, swan. The girl spent the day plucking the feathers of the swan, butchering the meat, but the brother asked for the delicate bones. This brother did not want to be a miller like his father. No, he was a storyteller who could sing and play, but he had broken his harp the week before. His father thought the broken harp would stop the young man's dreams, but the brother took the breastbone of the swan and made a harp out of it. When he finished, the harp played by itself.

"The brother traveled from hearth to hearth with his magical harp, and his renown grew. Soon lords and ladies heard of him and asked him to come and play for them. Finally, he was invited by the king and came before the court with his magical harp. As he made to sing with the harp, his voice was joined by the dead princess. He stopped singing while she told her story, the story of her jealous sister who killed to take her love. There in the court sat the elder princess with her new husband. She was hanged before the night was over."

"But what of the swan?"

"She remained in the care of her mother, the queen, and she would sit on a special chair while the queen sewed each day. She would sing to her mother and her mother would sing back to her. At first, the songs were all sad, but after a time, they learned new songs together, and they put away tears and chose happier things."

"The harp cried?" my mother asks in her wry voice.

"Well, one might suppose, because of the depth of sorrow in the songs, that the harp was crying as much as a harp can cry."

"I see." My mother's eyebrow lifts as she suppresses a smirk.

⁂

Perhaps I've been too tired to dream, but I was hoping, now that we are on our way to stop the sorceress, that the dreams had stopped because they were only nightmares—

nothing more. But as I sleep next to Paul, the visage of my witch appears, and above her looms a great dragon, dark purple and black, with a whipping tail. Its snout is elongated, and when it opens its mouth, the fire pours out like a river of purple flame. The witch turns to laugh at me; the fire surrounds her, but she does not burn. I can't breathe as the smoke enters my lungs, and the sound of her laughter fills my ears until I jerk awake, shaking in fear. I scoot closer to Paul, who puts his arm around me and mumbles in his sleep, "You all right?"

"Mmm-hmm," I respond, burrowing closer as though he can protect me from all that we are chasing.

⸙

As we near the mountains, a huge cliff juts up. Once we reach it, I am astounded by the sheer height of the craggy walls on either side of us. Unlike the bright white cliffs at the shore, these two cliffs are grey, reminding me of the stone used to make the Fisher King's castle.

Brother Jacob looks me in the face with the first full smile I have seen him wear. "It is in the face of something this grand that I feel the presence of God most." He has to shout to be heard over the roar of the waterfall as the Ventrias pours down from the mountains above. His smile is meant to be kind, I think, but I feel so small, like a tiny insect waiting to be crushed. Though I was surrounded by mountains at the High King's court, I did not feel this insignificant.

A glance up the grey of the cliff's walls reveals small trees growing in crevices. Ivy climbs, slowly making its way up higher and higher. It doesn't cover the entire face of either cliff, but somehow the plants give me comfort. How odd! It's as though because they are there, I can grow, too.

A mirthful laugh bubbles up inside me and I'm glad no one can hear my mind.

I look around at our small company. Though I am traveling among them, I am too much alone in my head at times. My thoughts were all I had, alone in my tower day after day. And when I was journeying this past year, there were only a few occasions I did not travel by myself. There was a short span of time in the company of others, the longest spent with Edmund's family. I think back on the carriage rides, which were much more comfortable than constantly feeling my horse shifting beneath me.

The waterfall roars as the river plummets from above. I can see my breath as we make our way behind the curtain of water. It feels otherworldly behind something moving at such speed. My heart quickens to think that if my horse were to slip, we would crash down to the rocks below.

Chilled, we emerge from behind the waterfall to face the steepest trail we have seen yet. At last I understand why our horses are so short and stocky. Their limber legs make quick work of the first incline, but I have to watch as Paul shows my mother and me how to lean forward in the saddle. It is a good thing he takes time while we are on our way to teach us better how to sit astride. I cannot imagine how I would be able to maintain my seat if I were sitting sidesaddle, as a proper lady would do.

Am I a proper lady? I have asked myself this question many times before. The answer remains the same even though my circumstances have changed. No. I have been alone most of my life and I feel glad to be with people—how I longed for it before!—but their very nearness, the way they so easily communicate with one another, it all feels like a riddle I have no answer to. Perhaps I should have stayed alone.

My eyes find Paul. I would not want him to know that I

have such thoughts, such doubts about my ability to live in his world. But surely, how can I become a proper queen if I am like this now? How can I be a good wife to him? I wonder if all brides feel this unsure in the first week they are wed. Though, of course, most brides would have known their wedding date and been prepared for it.

AT REST

oday is Sunday, and Jacob says we must rest every Sunday. It is good for the animals to do so, and I know that my body needs it, too. We each take time to wash our hands and faces in the river, but these mountain waters are cold! I can't submerge myself, though I ache to. Oh, to be able to bathe! Still, I get as clean as I can and finally get to let my raw feet soak for a bit. My thoughts linger on how fortunate we are to be traveling alongside the Ventrias. The sound of the water takes my mind off of darker thoughts. Lately, the fear that the king will die before we can help him and Paul, as his heir, will grow ill has blossomed like a poisonous flower in my thoughts.

Worrying over such things will not aid us; it is beyond my control. I should instead concentrate on what I can do, each step that I can take. A moan escapes me when Paul comes up behind me and begins kneading my shoulders with his strong hands.

"Thank you." I try to pull away, embarrassed, but he pulls me closer.

"Hold still, you obviously need this."

"I wouldn't need it if I could just take a hot bath."

"I don't imagine you had many since you left your tower."

I frown. "Not until I traveled through Rona." I regret bringing up Rona again; his hands have stopped their massage.

"I suppose you had a great many comforts while you were with the royal family."

"Most of the time, except when I was accused of murder and locked in the dungeon."

His hands stop again and he turns me to himself. "Who would accuse you of such a thing?"

I don't really want to think of how Edmund's father had believed the accusations, how Edmund used the power of his wish to free me. Such things are best unsaid, but Paul looks concerned. I suppose I would be, too, if I felt he were keeping something from me as well. I am tempted to speak, but then I think of how the last few mornings he and Brother Jacob have gone off to discuss things.

Is this the way between a man and a woman? Should we go to bed harboring secrets, keeping buried inside all the thoughts and fears, hoping the other will never find out and reject us? His eyes are clear, not angry; perhaps I should tell him. It seems a small thing. "There was an incident in one of the kingdoms we visited."

"During the summer, when the king was introducing Edmund to his lords?"

"Yes."

"And preparing them for you to be their queen."

I squirm a bit. "Yes. I had a maidservant and she died from a potion I was accused of giving her."

"Why would anyone accuse you?"

"I did give it to her, but I had been told it was a love potion."

"Why would you have a—" But he stops himself. He doesn't really want to know, does he? "How did it kill her?"

"The witch had transformed it."

His face reddens in anger. "She was trying to kill you?"

"She said it wouldn't have killed me. It was a way to cause me to cry out to her."

"But you didn't, did you?"

"No."

"Then, how—?"

"Edmund saved me."

He frowns and looks away from me. "I suppose that altered your feelings for him?"

"It did. He scared me. I worried he would use his power one day for evil. I suppose he already had, and he did so again when he wished me to marry him."

He nods, but he still can't look at me. Edmund feels present, his control a chasm gaping between us.

"I'm glad I know now that I have a will of my own."

He finally looks at me and takes a deep breath. "I would certainly say that you have a will of your own." He smiles at last, as though putting Edmund behind us. This is the smile I love, the one that crinkles his eyes. I reach up and pull his head down to mine and let my lips linger on his.

"What was that for?"

"Because you love *me*, not what you can make of me."

He removes my wimple and plays with my hair. Perhaps I'll stop wearing it now that I live in the North-lands. "Do you think it will ever grow as long as it was before?"

"No, and it's best it doesn't. I can't imagine trying to track it with me as we traipse around."

"Once we are settled in the Fisher King's castle, you might let it grow again."

I shake my head. "Longer than it is now, yes, but never as long as she made it grow before. I don't want anything to weigh me down again."

"Nothing ever will," he says as he bends lower to me to kiss me. His lips part and I feel that same thrill inside that I did the first night we kissed, the night he promised to return and take me far outside her reach. The night before I lost him. I kiss him harder, but then we break apart, as Amis has stumbled upon us.

"It's time to eat." He smiles in his odd little way. With anyone else I might feel put out. It is seldom I can be alone with Paul, to have a conversation with him and feel as though we are understanding one another. But I cannot be angry with Amis. There is something so childlike, so winsome in his manner.

THE TALE OF A CAT

e follow Amis back to where we've made camp and see that we have the rabbits that Paul and Jacob bought in a market town yesterday. I wonder, how does it sit with a hunter, having to buy someone else's kill? I am grateful to have it and not the dried fish and stale bread that I have become so tired of. Instead, the rabbit is tender, roasted over the flames so that I can taste the smoke. Who knew that this funny man would have a way with food? He has certainly kept us laughing, helped us talk, aided us in so many more ways than I ever imagined he would when he first flipped his way into our group.

He hands my mother a leg of a rabbit and she smiles slightly. I wonder how she feels about eating rabbit. Surely it is not so different for her than eating a mouse, though eating a mouse sounds grotesque to me.

"It is your turn, m'lady," he says, encouraging her.

"My turn?"

"Haven't you noticed? We have all been taking turns talking around the fire in the evening. It is your turn."

She looks at me as though to say I have not yet taken a turn, but perhaps she thinks better of it since there is that hard thing that lies between us.

"If you want a story, I suppose I have collected a few since my time as a cat."

"I'm sure your time was quite strange."

"Indeed? Why would you say that?"

"How could it not be?"

She laughs. "I know where I will start. It was the first place the witch put me after she made me feline. It was an overcrowded kitchen. They wanted a cat to keep away the mice and they had a great many that kept me quite busy at first. After a while, I had taken care of the mice and they began to have to feed me. I had earned a warm and cozy place by the hearth in the winter. I didn't think to wonder why she wanted me there, not until the first night she made me return to her. Her questions were so odd, but she had such a nice fat mouse that I couldn't seem to refuse to help her get what she wanted."

"And what did she want?" Amis has finished serving and takes what's left of the rabbit.

"She wanted to know about the head cook—what he was like. He was a rough sort, always angry and fussing at his minions. Later, she asked questions about his lord, and I was able to scoot through the doors of the kitchen one day and endear myself to the nobleman. He had a soft spot for animals, you see. It was interesting to watch him with his spoiled son. There were so many places that she had me go, so many people she wanted to know about." She takes a moment to chew as she thinks where next to take the story.

I grew a fondness for the Dark Wood, which runs throughout much of Alleria. I came to the home of a family with more brothers than I bothered to count. It was not long before I realized why she sent me there. The mother of the home was foolish like I once was. Eufemia appeared one day and the woman accused her of trespassing. I think Eufemia showed up that way on purpose, to have an excuse to curse the sons with barrenness. You met them later, Rapunzel."

"The family with all the brothers, and no children borne to any of them—Helga's family," I say, my throat tightening. "I remember they decided to find the witch and bargain. I didn't realize she was *my* witch."

My mother nods with sorrow. "It is wrong to sacrifice a child for any reason, but they agreed to give her the first-born if she would remove the curse. After that, Eufemia sent me into a different part of the Wood. It was deeper, darker, and I became lost. I felt cold and hungry when an old woman invited me inside her home. She made me welcome and treated me as kindly as though I had been her favorite child. She talked to me every day until at last I found myself answering back."

Amis is smiling, I imagine he is composing a song in his head with bits of my mother's life. "Did you not usually answer back?"

"No, I learned quite early in my feline life that if I answered back, I got hurt—kicked, thrown, one man tried to drown me. I finally decided that the best way to learn what the witch wanted to know was to listen very carefully and to act like the cat I appeared to be."

She has finished her leg, but she holds the bone absent-mindedly, gesturing with it on occasion. "It became easier as the years went by. I even thought about having a litter of my own, but I could never reconcile myself to the idea that I might stay a cat forever. And I never aged as a cat should,

I just stayed the same year after year—except for the few times she would bring me to her to tell her things. Sometimes she would allow me to transform back almost entirely into the woman I once was . . . but I think she didn't do that out of kindness, I think it brought her a twisted happiness to see me writhe as I became Cat again."

The thought of my mother being tortured like this doesn't sit well with me. I hate it. The anger inside me for all she did long ago is being pushed far away from me so I won't feel it one day. It hurts—it hurts far more than I could have imagined. But I would rather think only of what is being said in this moment.

She continues on. "The old woman's name was Dorothea, and she had a strange secret. She was helping God, as his servant, and she had a room of sorting. You've been there, Rapunzel."

My mouth hangs open. "Yes."

"In that room, those who are grief-stricken come and find a way to make peace with what went wrong in their life. Then they can leave the room and the Deep Wood and discover that God works all things together for good of those who are called to be his."

I close my mouth.

"What Dorothea didn't know was that, in that room, there was a man who was trapped in his grief and wouldn't leave. The witch wanted him to stay there, to keep others from seeing the goodness of God, the trustworthy nature of his plans."

"Nicholas?" I breathe the question.

"He lost his wife just after their twins became a year old. Dorothea could never help him move forward, and she told him he would have to leave or forever be frozen in his grief. She thought he did leave, but it was a trick of the witch. She used me to deceive her."

"Some things don't need explaining," I murmur, remembering what Dorothea had said to me once when I was trying to understand her and how her service to God and others worked.

Paul is looking at my mother in a strange way. "I feel as though there is something about you . . ."

She laughs at his expression. "I wondered when or if you would remember."

"Remember what?" I can't stop myself from jumping in.

"What do you remember, dear son?" Her eyes are creasing in smile.

"I don't know. It's as though you were in that other half-life that the witch had me living. You weren't, though, were you? It's just my mind trying to—sometimes I can remember bits and pieces of it as though it were gone like my normal life. After I began to remember Rapunzel, that half-life began to fade and I remember so little of it. But at times, hazy memories of it come back. It's as though it's part of a dream."

A shudder shakes me as the thought of the lying life I led while under Edmund's second wish invades my mind. If only I couldn't remember how I had felt, how I had acted. I want it to have happened to a different person and the decisions I made then erased forever. But it had been me—I had allowed him to choose things for me, I had changed for him and not been true to who I was supposed to be.

My face lowers as I look at the ground. I feel so scarred by him—no, not scarred—raw and ragged, as though this place inside me is still bleeding. There is a wound here, and some of it is because of what Edmund did, but a great deal of it is guilt over what I did, what I allowed him to do. Why can't I release the past? I am with Paul now—

shouldn't that fix things? This choice—my choice—should have made it all better! I want to run away, find a crevice in the rocks and cry, weep for the time we lost. I feel as though I betrayed myself, though I know it was out of ignorance.

Paul's voice lifts my eyes and I return from my morose reverie. "There was a calico that would come through the stables. There she would be one day, mousing and hunting. I liked her. I loved to scratch behind her ears and—" A look of pure shock crosses his face as a wide smile stretches my mother's lips apart until laughter bursts from beneath her sorrow. "You talked to me!"

"Only when no one else was around." The fire continues to snap and crackle as darkness gathers.

"I remember you talking to me. I thought I had lost my mind!"

"Well, I suppose it is understandable that you would feel that way."

"When did you begin talking to me?"

"Not at first, but after you began noticing me, it was easy to find time to follow you around. Every once in a while you would be alone. The first time I spoke to you, I thought you might run and hide."

Paul is laughing. "I was that terrified!"

"True, but you didn't run. You stayed and asked who I was."

"I remember now—you said that you were the one who could tell me who I really was. You told me such strange stories each time I saw you, but—" He looks confused again, bewildered, which is a funny expression on him.

My mother licks her lips. "I had to begin again each time I saw you, re-explain everything to you. I had to tell you again who you were, where you had come from. I kept trying to tell you about Rapunzel, how you needed to go find her—"

"Why wouldn't I listen?"

"Because your enchantment was so strong. Also, I think Eufemia placed me there simply to make certain I could see how hopeless it all was."

I lean forward. "Do you think she knew that I would one day run into Paul?"

"I think it is entirely possible. She had reason to be acquainted with the goings-on in Rona. She had a way with the kingdoms and she had her hand in many things Ute was wanting. She was their tool and you were hers, just as I was hers."

"But not forever." I sigh. She was not able to maintain her power forever.

"No, of course not, the God of heaven and earth would never allow such a thing."

"But why would he allow it at all?" I can't help questioning.

My mother stares at me. "What do you mean?"

"If he is so powerful and so strong, why would he allow any of this to happen?" I know I'm not just asking about my own plight. I am wondering about Adeliza's dead child, Ysentrude's love, the curse we are fighting in the Northlands. "Why would the God of heaven and earth who you say is so good also allow such bad things to happen?"

Jacob speaks with his firm voice while shadows flicker over his face in the firelight. "Rapunzel, do you believe in our God?"

I have not had anyone ask this of me outright in a very long time. "I don't know how to believe, sir. I was not raised to it and I am not comfortable with the idea of it. These questions keep at me, stinging me relentlessly."

Jacob surprises me by his gentle laughing. "Yes, why?"

"You mock me?"

"I understand you, I echo you."

"But you are a monk, a priest yourself."

"I wasn't born one. Yes, I fight for God and who he is, but I still have doubts."

"How can you reconcile living a life for a God you aren't sure of?"

"But I am sure of him."

I shake my head and sputter. "I don't—what do you mean? You aren't sure of him, but you are? How—what?"

"I know in the deepest part of myself that God is bigger and more infinite than I can fathom. I have witnessed and experienced personally his grace, his faithfulness, his steadfast love. I have also seen and known things that have shaken me and made me doubt. Each doubt I take to his feet in prayer."

"To his feet?"

"We are told in scripture to bring our requests before his throne, so I picture myself coming into his court. There I lie prostrate on the ground, whispering my requests, laying them in front of me before his feet."

I think on this image. I think of God on his throne. Would it be huge, massive, with a banner behind it? What colors would the God of heaven have for himself? What kind of army would he have fighting for him? Would it be full of monks like Jacob, trained like my Paul?

I have heard it said God's angels are not just messengers, but also warriors. Are they like this monk—fierce, strong, loyal? Are they like Paul—tall, thoughtful, protective? My eyes glance over at Amis and I wonder if any of them are funny. Is God funny? Does he have a sense of humor? I look at my mother and think of myself. Are any of us not ridiculous? God must have a sense of humor to have put us together. I suppose I do believe God is real, but what do I believe about him? Do I trust him? I think everyone else around this fire does, though it turns out they have doubts, too. Surprising.

THE PATH AHEAD

My heart skips as I see the next steep incline that we will be taking. There to the left is another fork that meanders into the mountain. I wish Paul would choose that route, though I understand why we can't. The path looks gentle with its rising slope gradually inclining. The path is grey like the rock, and pretty wide. Perhaps two of us could venture side by side into it. I like the idea of being next to someone—it sounds safer.

Instead, we take the steeper path. We journey on, and I feel my body straining as though I can help Honey move forward. I watch Paul closely and mimic how he leans, how he encourages his horse. We have to stop a few times to wait for each other while our horses navigate a trickier bit of the trail. It is start and stall, start and stall. I can't seem to find my rhythm today. The height is distracting and I fear I will tumble over, perhaps even fall off the edge of the cliff.

What if Paul is wrong and we shouldn't be going this way? The other path is well-worn by those who bring things to trade between the Fisher King and King Onfroi.

I try not to worry, but I keep shifting from side to side trying to help the horse. Paul is up already at the top of this last stretch and looks pained. "Relax, Rapunzel, you're doing fine." I'm sweating and gripping the reins so hard. I take a deep breath to try to settle my heart's rapid pace. The mare grunts as she stumbles and teeters to the side. I release my grip with a gasp as Honey stumbles. I fall to the side and tumble down part of the mountain, battered on reaching a flat stretch.

I lay in a heap, wishing I could be unconscious. Amis is the first to reach me, and then my mother. "Hold still," she advises, and begins checking me over.

"What are you doing?"

"Making certain your bones aren't broken."

I bite back that she hasn't been in human form long enough in the last two decades to really know what broken bones are like. While she is still doing this, Jacob joins us and at last Paul makes it over to me and hovers nearby.

"Rapunzel! Is she okay?"

My mother tries to help me sit up, and a sharp pain in my side makes me suck in my breath with a cry. "Where does it hurt?"

I motion to my ribs without speaking, and she cautiously probes where I gesture.

"You've cracked a rib, but you're lucky it wasn't worse."

I stare at her in pain, wondering how she knows to check for such things.

Jacob shakes his head. "I've had my share of cracked ribs. I do not envy you the journey ahead."

My mother is tearing off a wide swath of material from her chemise. "I need to bind her ribs. Rapunzel, come with me." The men scatter as we find some privacy behind some trees. "Forgive me, daughter, this will hurt."

I raise my hands to remove my dresses and a lightning bolt of pain pierces my side. I blink against dark spots in my vision. My mother helps steady me so I don't pass out and then wraps the cloth around my ribs as tight as I can stand. She gingerly pulls the dress layers over my head and then helps me walk. "It's going to hurt, possibly for months, but you'll get used to it. I'm sorry, Rapunzel. I wish we could find a place for you to rest for a few days."

I think of the growing chill in the air and the invalid king. There is no time to just rest. We must journey on.

Honey's screeching whinny startles me, which brings on more pain as I jerk toward the sound. We find the men standing over the downed horse, where Paul is removing his bloodied sword from her side. His eyes look up in sorrow. "She broke her leg, and there is no mending such an injury for a horse. I'm sorry, Rapunzel, but we will make do. You'll have to ride with me." But he doesn't have any of us mount again for the remainder of the day. Instead, with a great deal of help (and much internal moaning on my part) we climb the rest of the incline on foot. The horses take a great deal of soothing, but once we get started, each person leads their horse. The pack animals are still tied to Jacob's and Amis' horses, and it takes a long time to regain our lost ground. Since Paul is in the lead, I am able to stop and rest while the others are still climbing.

⚬⚬⚬

BY THE TIME we find a flat clearing, it is evening and we are exhausted. I settle down to rest as Paul and Jacob brush the horses down and Amis starts the fire. Despite the pain that throbs with each breath, the fool's humming calms me. The horses chomp and snort when the brushing is through and refresh themselves as they graze on the grass growing by the banks of the Ventrias.

When Jacob prays before we eat, I find his prayers remind me of the witch's incantations. But in his voice there is an entreaty, whereas she sounded commanding. Does one have to know just the right words to persuade this God to do what you want done? But it seems there is more to prayer than that, even in the little experience I've had with it.

Paul gathers blankets for our bedding and lays them out upon the ground so that I don't have to. I lie down, and I try resting my head on his chest by lying on my right side, his left arm beneath me. But the sharp pain takes my breath away and I have to lie still on my back, tears gathering in my eyes. Paul turns on his side and places a protective arm over me. "I'm sorry you hurt, my love." His musky scent fills my senses, and I would that I could kiss him with abandon, to make all the pain in my body come to a stop.

"There is something bothering you, more than just your ribs. What is it?" His voice is low so the others won't hear.

I can't help thinking of the sorceress who visits in my dreams, but I can't have him knowing that. "The first night we set out I asked my mother about my father. I have never even known his name."

"What was it?" Paul knows how he died.

"Guarin. She said I look like him—well, my hair does. I never knew that either. My mother grew up on a goat farm and made cheese." My voice deepens; a scratchy quality enters my sharing. "I—I thought I had forgiven them both, Paul, my mother and my witch." I stop talking, I hate the swelling of my throat that threatens tears are coming.

Paul strokes my hair. I've given up on wearing the wimple. He somehow manages not to get his fingers caught in the curls. "It is hard to forgive. It's something we can't do on our own."

My face pinches. I'm not sure what he means . . . and I'm not sure I want to know.

"I have had to work hard with God's help to forgive my own father, and I fear I will never be done with the task."

"Your father?" My voice comes out in a burst of shock.

"Rapunzel, perhaps it is shameful to say it, but my father is not a good man. He is a strong king, he rules his people fairly, he takes care of the matters of court and trade, but I'll never understand how he gets along with my uncle. They are—different. My uncle would never—" But here he stops. I have never heard such a rush of heat in his tone before. I begin to turn to get a better look at him, but cry out in pain.

"Shhh! Be still, my love." He kisses my lips, but I don't forget my question.

"What has he done to make you feel this way? I have never heard you speak ill of him."

"I try never to do so. As I said, he is a king, but he is also just a man . . ." His voice trails off. "I would rather not speak of it. It's been a long day."

I can't help thinking of all the things I left unasked, unsaid during our courtship. I spent the past year mourning him, wishing we had spoken of the details of his life. There is still so much of him that I don't know, that I don't understand. Sometimes he speaks and shares, but here he is, shutting me out. What am I to do about that?

"Paul, please talk to me. Please tell me what happened."

"Rapunzel, I can't." His voice strains as he turns onto his back and points up. "Look at the night sky, see how the stars glow? Let's gaze on that, instead, until we go to sleep. We have a long journey ahead of us, and we need our rest."

Perhaps he is right; he has gone into the mountains before, whereas I never have. I swallow salty tears chilling my flushed face, but are they caused by the pain in my ribs or in my heart? I don't know how to be his wife, do I?

I will myself to relax. His body stills except for the rising and falling of his chest which shifts our blanket a bit as he breathes in and out. My head longs to rest on his chest and feel the thump of his heart again. I know it would help lull me to sleep, help me know I am safe and we will find our way to live as man and wife. Won't we?

Instead, I spend hours awake, staring into the bit of grey the half-moon allows me to see.

TAKING TURNS

It's a tricky thing, climbing up onto a horse after cracking a rib. The only way I will manage this morning is to accept that, no matter how careful I am, there is going to be horrible pain. Paul swings onto his horse and then helps me up into his lap as I sit sidesaddle. I have to be careful to tuck myself as close to Paul as possible, as he has his sword in a sheath hanging on the front of the saddle. He won't be able to draw it out with me sitting here, but I hope that he wouldn't need to, anyway. When Paul clicks his tongue and shifts his body while holding the reins properly, his mare responds by heading up the trail. I hold my breath until I get used to his mare's movement, thankful for the binding that my mother wound around my ribs this morning.

My view this morning is more of the scenery instead of the hind end of a horse. It makes for a pleasant change. Having Paul's arms around me hurts my side, but I know it must be borne. He is not the sort of man that must talk to fill the silence, which is nice. I spend much of the morning watching squirrels that scamper from tree to tree, some of them leaping at such a distance that they fairly seem to glide through the air. Wonder fills me at their bustle. The flying *v*'s of flocks of geese soar high above us again. The weather continues to cool, and I delight in the hues of autumn surrounding us.

⬙⬙

"IT IS YOUR TURN, RAPUNZEL," Amis says as he hands me my portion of dried provisions.

I groan and the others laugh. We sit around the fire like we do any night we don't find a home or inn to rest in. Amis serves us and then sits over to one side, feeding the fire until we rest. I usually sit at his right, and Paul at my right, then there is Jacob to his right, and my mother completes the circle, often right across the flames from me.

"I don't really have any stories to tell that you don't already know," I mumble and take a bite in order to not have to say anything more.

"There is a great deal from your life that we don't know."

"Such as?"

"What was it like growing up with a witch for a mother?"

"She wasn't my mother," I say quickly, wanting to snuff out the hurt on my mother's face.

"But she was like a mother to you," my mother states simply. Her face is downcast despite the warm orange glow provided by the fire.

"That is true, I suppose," I concede, and take another bite to give myself time. "She was kinder to me when I was younger. There were times that she made me laugh, and we loved to tell each other stories. Mine were made up, but hers were complicated. She loved to tell me over and over again of how people would steal from her.

"I think it was a warning, that she would not allow someone to take what was hers. As I got older, she put me in the tower, and I realized she thought of me as hers. I was something that belonged to her, something she owned. She was protecting me from the world of men, she would say, but really, she was protecting me from being taken.

"Her tales were stories of warnings, and many were about sisters. I thought about those stories more and more when I was traveling around Rona. We had long carriage rides as we went from place to place to meet the lords and ladies. I didn't know then that she was a protege of Ute—I didn't even know there *were* sisters of sorcery. But she loved to tell of men who tried to control women. Wasn't that what she did with me? She tried to control me, tried to keep me from deciding what it was that I wanted in my life."

Now that I have opened my mouth, the words keep coming. I stare into the flames, hypnotized by my own story. "Choosing was difficult because I didn't think I had choices at first. I lived in a house with a wall around it, then I lived in a tower with no doors. When I came to the world, there were wide, unbroken places where my feet could run, but where would I go? I knew she wanted me to not know what to do, so I just went. I met friends, but I couldn't make up my mind to stay anywhere, I couldn't decide to trust anyone. I still—" I can't say that out loud. It's as though I've been talking to myself all this time, but now I see their faces all around me. I don't know what they are thinking. I listen to the snapping of the flames.

"Was she ever kind?" Amis nudges me back to talking.

"Sometimes. She used to sing to me. She taught me some happy songs. Others were sad. There were strange ones with odd words. I didn't really like those, but I can't seem to forget them."

Paul frowns at this. "I never heard you singing those."

"I don't, they always make me feel—"

"Sing one." Jacob's voice is low, it has a growl inside it.

I look at Paul and he nods. With my stomach turning sour I begin to sing in a minor key the eerie tune that travels up and down, the vowels and consonants stringing together in a moan.

"Stop!" the monk cries out, coming over to me. "She taught you that?"

"Well, she sang it and others like it when I was young."

"Did she have you sing it back to her?"

"I wouldn't—I mean, I did at first, but as I grew older, I refused."

"What did she do?"

"She told me that was fine, but then she would laugh. I hated that laugh."

"Don't ever sing that song again, Rapunzel. It is as evil as you knew it to be."

Something in me shivers. I did not want to be right, but I was. The song was evil.

"What else did she teach you?"

My food is gone and I brush my lap free of crumbs as I shift on the blanket Paul placed on the rocky ground. "How to read and write—so many languages. Some of them she didn't teach me, she just gave me books and I had to figure it out for myself if I wanted something to read. She would give me little clues, like small riddles, and I would spend my days figuring out translations. She knew how to tease my mind to learn. I had no idea how important it would be until I began to travel outside my tower. I don't speak every language, but it has been fun to hear some of them spoken aloud." I lean forward with a smile.

"For instance, I find it fascinating to hear the sounds of how the Northlanders pronounce things and how the Allerians speak. I have not been to the Eastern Ports, of course, but I met people like you, Brother Jacob, and I think I could learn your language with little difficulty. It is very close to Latin, I think."

Have I been babbling, all my thoughts just flowing into one another? Paul looks amused, but Jacob's brow is furrowed. "The two languages are very similar, and most of us from the Ports speak both fluently. Tell me, of what use would your knowledge of so many languages be to your witch?"

"Use? It was just a way to occupy me. She wanted me to have some sort of entertainment, especially after she wouldn't allow me to garden anymore."

The silence that gathers after I say this is telling, but what it says I cannot decipher.

⚬

AFTER OUR DAY OF REST, I feel stiff and groan at the chill. I start to stamp around this morning in order to get warm, but moan as a sharp pain shoots up my side. I should have known better! The horse's breath is visible in the air as Paul pats his mare and uses his low voice to speak calming words to her. Then he looks at us. "The next few days, the path will continue to be steep. We will do what we first did, walking parts of it to give the horses and us a break." He sounds sure of himself, and then he looks back to Jacob. The monk gives a slight nod of approval, but his lips are back in that firm line.

Learning to lean forward while sitting in his lap with a cracked rib hurts, but I'm struggling to do it anyway. I get nervous and try not to look down over the side of the mountain. The distance we've come is huge in such a short amount of time. When I look over the side, my stomach gives a strange flip and I don't like it at all. Paul, behind me, is coming alive, his voice suddenly boisterous and occasionally breaking into song.

"Don't tense like that, relax." Paul scolds. "It's a good thing you're not holding the reins, you'd be holding her back and slowing us down." I give him a look over my shoulder. "I'm sorry, I forget that you are still new at this."

I don't want to be the reason we can't complete this mission in time to save the kings. My lips smile at him and then I take a deep breath. We dismount, and for the next hour we walk. I am grateful I'm able to stretch a bit, but I stumble a bit, causing another lightning bolt of pain. How can I hurt this much? I try to think of things to count as blessings: warm clothes, good husband, beautiful trees. But the more I ache, the more I cringe at the thought of all that looms beyond. My eyes look ahead; the top of the mountain seems out of reach.

THE TALE OF A WARRIOR MONK

My mother has taken to checking on me. The bruising around my ribs is a deep purple with fingers of green and brown slowly spreading outward as the days travel forward. "How did you know what to do?" I ask at last, staring at her as she binds me once more behind some trees.

"I was training to be a midwife, back before . . . Your father's mother was a kind widow who cared for all the people near us, and she was teaching me her craft. I was mostly interested in bringing new life into the world, but healing was something I was also learning. I wonder what my life would have been like, had I not sinned against my sister." She shakes her head and tries to smile at me.

"Perhaps you can resume your studies, when we finish our quest."

She laughs. "I'd not thought that far ahead. This journey we are on, I have a hard time seeing its completion." Her eyes meet mine for a moment, but we break away from one another. Some things are too difficult to discuss.

Except for the pain in my side every time I take a breath, the day passes uneventfully and we make camp under several tall trees.

We sit around the fire as the smell of roasting nuts makes our mouths water. All of us look a bit tired, but Amis has a way of drawing even the quietest among us out. "What was your family like?" he asks Jacob, who looks up from shelling a walnut.

"I was given to the Church for my mother's sins."

I notice my mother starts at this and stares at our warrior monk, but Amis takes no notice as he continues pulling the story from Jacob. "Were you taken from her?"

"My mother was a witch. She did not set out to do evil, but she was consumed with having her own way in many things and became entangled by others who secretly consulted dark spirits in the swamps of the Eastern Ports. When my father realized what she was doing, he took her to the Church, and her penance was to give me up."

Amis frowns. "Do you remember her?"

Jacob shakes his head. "She gave me up at birth, so I never knew family life as many of you have."

That sounds familiar to me. I notice that Paul is looking my way as though he knows this story is close to my pain.

"Did you always know about your mother?"

Jacob chews thoughtfully for a moment before replying. "No, of course not. I lived in ignorance for a long time. When I was a young man I received the call of God on my life. I knew that I should become a monk, but in order to do so, my priest insisted that I knew why I had been given to the Church. When I heard the truth, I became ill. How could I serve a God who had separated me from my mother? How could I serve a God who had *given* me such a mother?"

I can't help the glance I steal at my mother. Our eyes lock for a moment and then we both look away.

Amis hands out more nuts he has finished roasting, and we set to work shelling once they have cooled off. "What did you do?"

"I concentrated more on the warrior side of my training, discovering through sweat and training with weapons that I could pour out my anger and fears to God. It was as though the fighting released something deep within me, and I could pray as I never had before. If it had not been for the priest's telling me the truth, I might never have confronted the anger and fear that were deep within me. I might never have discovered the depth of God's love for me. Neither height nor depth nor darkness can keep us from the love of God. It abounds more than we can fathom."

"He is not scared of our questions," Paul murmurs, and I know it is for my ears alone, to tuck deep within. He might not remember, but I remember him saying this before, back when I lived isolated in my tower. I didn't know what to do with it then—or what to do with it now. How can I ask God all the things that are burdening my heart if I don't even know if I trust in him? What if my faltering faith that he might be real is wrong? Would I just be talking to myself if he doesn't exist?

I feel ashamed. I am not the only one who has had a difficult life or a strange upbringing. Others in this small group have struggled. I try to settle down for the night, still finding it difficult to find a position that doesn't hurt. Paul lies on his side, once more guarding me with his strength, but after a time he turns over in his sleep. I sigh, get up softly, and move away from camp as quietly as possible.

I look up through the branches of a tree that has already begun to shed its leaves. I see the flecks of starlight in the sky, and I lift my voice in a whisper to the God I want to trust.

"I don't know what you want from me, God, and I don't even know that I believe you are real. But if it is you that has led me all along, and not just the witch or this sorceress, then show me who I am and who I was made to be.

"I have been told that you have a plan for my life. I don't really like that. It's not as though I know what I want for my life. It's just—I don't think I like that you have something that you want for me and from me. Maybe if I knew I could trust you, if I knew that you were for me . . . Paul says that you love me, Adeliza said that you died for me, Queen Lefwenna said you forgave me . . . I do admit that if you are real, I am deeply flawed and need that forgiveness.

"Still, I don't know how to feel about you. What do you want from me? Will it consume all of me? I'm not sure I want to be consumed by you. What will be left if you do?"

My voice fades into the darkness and I hear something behind me rustle. Pale moonlight reflects off the image of my cloaked mother. Of all our company, I know that she is the only one that I would be okay with hearing this prayer, though I don't know why. Perhaps it is because I feel certain we hold our faith in the same way, with confusion and fear.

"It is good that you have prayed." Her voice is low, but steady.

An owl hoots before I answer in a shaky whisper, "Is it?"

"Yes."

"Why?"

"Prayer shows that you have hope—or that you *want* to have hope. God will use it in your life, Rapunzel."

I shift, scattering leaves with my feet. "Have you prayed?"

"Every day since I found you. Do you find that surprising?"

"Yes, I didn't imagine you were the praying sort."

"I never used to be, but now—I think I am supposed to be his, though I'm not sure that I really can be after the life I've led."

I look down in the darkness, away from her cat-like stare. I cannot answer her. I don't know why God would want to spend time with any of us.

THE DRAGON'S BREATH

We wake to the acrid smell of smoke drifting over the mountains the next morning. Screams echo from somewhere up ahead. We bundle ourselves in haste and mount, riding into we know not what. A roar shakes the ground, and above the trees we see a dragon swoop down, its purple scales shining in morning's light.

Paul holds the reins with his left hand and his sword with the other. He and Jacob and Amis ride on ahead, leaving my mother and me behind with her horse and the pack animals. "We have to stay calm," my mother says firmly. We stand with the horses, gripping the reins, cloaks over their heads to keep them still—which proves challenging with a dragon flying through the sky.

The black eyes—Ute's eyes!—are huge in the dragon's face, and though she breathes her flames above us, she does not come any closer. She shrieks again and then disappears, leaving no trace. The men return to us and we ride without stopping, grateful the horses have settled, until we reach the destruction.

The sun is high overhead when we reach a burned-out husk of a town. Our horses stamp the ground and look around as though to tell us they don't want to stay. The smoke is thick and I can't help coughing. There are trees and buildings still smoldering. Despite the look of horror on the faces of those in the street helping the wounded, I feel the conviction that this was nowhere near as bad as it could have been. There are several buildings that have been destroyed by fire, and their charred remains are testaments that something has gone horribly wrong. Paul dismounts and helps me down, and again I can't help the sharp intake of breath at the pain.

My mother takes the lead, going through our clean clothes and ripping them apart to make bandages. She directs Amis to refill the bladders with fresh water, and she helps clean wounds while Jacob works by her side, blessing those dying. The burn victims are the worst. The smell of roasted flesh now oozing with blood is horrific to behold. My eyes smart, but I listen to her instructions, try to help as best I can.

We start a fire to ward off the cold and share our blankets, but by morning it is apparent that most won't survive. We stay for days, trying to help, trying to heal, but the devastation is complete. After a week, we light a pyre to burn the corpses before we head away.

⌘

I'VE ALLOWED my mind to wander this evening, dwelling on my fears. I can't ignore my sore bits and pieces. If only I could take a soothing bath in the river—even if it is cold and I might be carried downstream to a waterfall by the rapid current! But Jacob says *no* and Paul agrees. He always agrees with Jacob.

We wash ourselves the best we can but must not immerse ourselves in the cold. What's wrong with me? Even though I can get clean this way, I don't feel clean. Is it the idea of being alone to bathe myself? If only I could have a few moments away, to think things through. I can't stop seeing the image of the dragon. I can't stop hearing the voice of the sorceress.

I startle back to reality when Amis creeps back into our camp where we are sitting and furtively motions to Paul. The men jerk to their feet, aware of something that I'm not. The horses hobbled nearby stamp, their nerves taut.

Suddenly, I'm grabbed from behind. The smell of human filth clings to him as his blade nicks my throat. "Throw it down!" he bellows behind me, my ears feeling as though they will split. Paul drops the sword he unsheathed and Amis the knife he just whipped out. "Go stand before the fire, you, two. You, woman, join them!" he yells at my mother. The blade is sharp and it bites deeper into my skin. "I'm cutting her and I'll cut her more. MOVE!" They begin shifting in front of the fire.

THWACK! I feel the man crumple as a staff crashes against his skull. His grip on the knife falters, but not before he has cut me again. I put a hand to my wound, and my mother rushes towards me. She rips another piece of her chemise beneath her layers of gowns to staunch the blood.

"I suppose things could be worse," my mother states, but her voice shakes.

"A poor place to get a cut." Amis remarks as he leaves us to go settle the horses with soft pats and low words. "I suppose, if we need to, we can tie that cloth around her neck, but it might have an unfortunate side effect."

I try to laugh. My mother is right: things could be worse. Paul looks dismayed, though, and almost glares at

Brother Jacob as the warrior says, "This is just the begin-ning, I feel it."

❧

"WHAT DID HE MEAN, 'This is just the beginning'?" I ask Paul in a whisper once he has come back to our bed from watching the prisoner a few hours. I couldn't sleep while he was up, too many thoughts swarming my mind.

"I'm not sure." Paul sounds irritated, and I can't understand why.

"Oh," I breathe out, sure he is withholding something from me. Is he pushing me away? How can I be important to what we are doing, what we are trying to accomplish, if he won't share with me what he is thinking? Brother Jacob is quite happy to make most of the decisions when Paul struggles, and Paul wants no counsel from me. This is not how I imagined things at all. We need to work together, and we can only do that if—

I hear a movement and see that my mother has gotten up from her place. She is walking away from our little camp. I suppose she is going to relieve herself, but I don't like to see her going off by herself after this evening. Paul has turned his back to me. I rise quietly. "I'll just be a moment," I state, and wander after my mother.

"Mother?"

There is a pause before her answer, and her voice is strained in the darkness. I wish I could see her face. "Yes?"

"Are you quite well?"

"As well as I can be."

I don't like this answer. It's as though she wants to say something, but won't. "How is that?"

"It is as I've said."

Wonderful! So now the two people I love most in all the

world won't speak to me. They won't share with me the problems that are dominating their thoughts. What is keeping them from speaking the truth?

Something wriggles inside of me. Have I been entirely truthful with them? Aren't there things I should tell them? I shove these things back, imagining for a moment that I am as fierce as Brother Jacob was when he came up behind that thief and knocked him out. That must be an amazing feeling, to be strong and able to protect those you are with. I stare into the gloom where I know my mother is sitting and imagine that if she were still a cat, I would at least be able to see her eyes.

"Leave me, Rapunzel. Give me time."

But time for what? There are moments when I fear that I will never understand anyone around me. They are each such a mystery and always wanting something. No matter how I try, I can't ever seem to understand what that *something* is.

I retreat back to my blanket next to Paul and think of turning my back to him as he did to me. Instead, I carefully fit my body next to his back and put my arm around him. I suck in a deep breath, pretending I don't feel the stab in my ribs. After a moment he turns to me. "I'm sorry." His voice is husky and deep.

"For what?" I ask in ignorance.

"I should have protected you. You are my wife, not his."

I don't mean to laugh, but I do. He is only angry at himself! "Beloved, I know you would have found a way to save me, but Jacob was in a position to do so before you. That is all. Wouldn't you say that it was God who allowed this to take place?"

"What do you mean?"

"I'm not really sure. It's something you have said to me

before, that God wills certain things and he allows certain things. Perhaps he has some reason for allowing Jacob to save me this time."

"This time?" He reaches around me and pulls me tightly into his hard chest and I cry out. "I'm sorry, did I hurt you?"

I have to turn onto my back to calm the screaming pain. "A bit." I take several breaths while Paul situates himself on his side to look at me.

"Are you planning on getting into danger again?"

"Well, I didn't do it on purpose!" I protest, but I can't help laughing when he tickles me, and then I cry out in pain again.

"I'm sorry!" He stops, but not before kissing my mouth. We can hear the others shift in their sleep. Or perhaps they can't sleep with us making so much noise. "I love you, Rapunzel, and I want you to stay as safe as possible."

"It's not as though that will be easy on this journey—though if I would stop falling off horses and getting captured by thieves, that might help. I imagine you'll be able to keep me safe for the rest of our days once we find the source of Ute's power—once we cut her off and heal the kings." I stare where I think I can see his face, and it looks like he might be smiling. An owl hoots and I hear a scuffle nearby in the branches. I imagine leaves skittering to the ground as the wind picks up.

"Most kings and queens stay their whole lives in castles or on their grounds taking in a hunt. Here we are, wandering off into the mountains to defeat a sorceress."

"I suppose we will find our way, as long as it is together."

He kisses me and I find that I want more of him. His kiss reminds me of the first night he kissed me, when we were still in the tower . . . before I knew my witch had discovered us . . . before he got thrown out of my life and was made to forget me. I hurt for that lost time, but what if in all that time away from him I was learning something? Could it be that in every hardship there is a lesson?

I have often felt as though there was a Great Hand guiding me, at times shielding me, but I'm not sure if that is the hand of God or the sorceress who invades my dreams now. Perhaps I am too weak. What if Paul and Jacob are wrong and her purpose is greater than God's? I close my eyes as though I can shut out these thoughts, but I cannot. I kiss Paul back and pretend to forget these worries.

THE SORCERESS SPEAKS

My witch is cackling, as she was wont to do. "What did you expect of marriage, my dear? To always get along?"

Where am I? Where did she come from? I am uncertain how to handle the sudden confusion that overwhelms me as I look around into the grey mist that surrounds me. "What have you done with him?" I ask the mirage of my witch.

"I haven't done anything with him, I'm not even alive anymore."

"No, but I am."

Behind me, I hear a voice. It is deep and reminds me of velvet. I feel someone standing behind me, and I turn to see her face. "Who are you?"

"You know who I am, sweet Rapunzel, just I have always known about you. Eufemia spoke of you and how she was training you. You didn't take well to her lessons, though, did you?"

"Training me?"

"All those hours in the garden, all those books of stories

—what do you think she was trying to do, just entertain you?"

I am speechless as I stare at her. She is tall and floats above me, her long gown of the darkest purple glittering like the night sky. I can't see her feet as the gown drips its length down to the ground. Her hair is white like my witch's, but looks smooth, almost glowing in the night, as though she is a star. Her eyes are pools of darkness, contrasting with her luminous skin. I feel pulled into her, but I resist her current.

"What do you want?"

"You know what I want—and now that you are coming, I will finally get it."

"I don't understand."

"But you will."

I hear crying, and her face splits into a sneering smile. "You think to rescue this land you must stand by his side." Her elegant hand points to where I can now see Paul sleeping. "No matter where you go or how you follow him, you will fail, and you will not be able to stop what I have set in motion. What you are doing now will only strengthen me —so by all means, come to me, find me, give me what I need to reunite myself with my sisters."

The sound of her laughter is different than my witch's; it is low and rumbles deep in her chest. As she begins to fade, I wake at once and shoot upright, startling Paul.

"What's wrong?"

I can't voice it. It is too odd, too strange. Dreams have long told me things, but they have also confused me. I won't let this one change our course of action. Is this the right thing to do? "Nothing, just a strange dream." I mutter.

⸎

"WHAT ARE we going to do with him now?" Jacob had the last watch of the night and was grateful when we awoke. I hadn't thought this far ahead. We have a prisoner, but also a journey to continue, a quest to complete. If we let him go, what might happen?

My mother steps forward and smiles at Jacob. "Let me talk to him." Her smile has a leering quality to it, but as I have begun to notice, Jacob seems to understand her.

"What is your name?" The man stares at my mother, his eyes glazed over, rhuemy. "He has a name, I'm sure of it." My mother laughs, and it reminds me of my witch. "Why won't you speak to our priest?"

The man blinks and turns his eyes toward her, but they aren't focused. "I have no reason to."

"I see. But will you talk to me?"

His head dips forward in a slight nod.

"Why?"

"You're different. You have the mark."

"What do you mean?"

His head lists to the side and he blinks again before finally answering. "It is clear you understand. You know what it is to have someone control you."

"Oh, have you been controlled?"

"Why else would I come after her?" He points his stubbly chin my way. "I don't want her for myself, but I had to get her."

"How do you mean?"

"I woke yesterday morning with a blinding headache. I couldn't see, the brightness of the sun was piercing."

My mother clucks her tongue and I imagine her batting playfully at a cat's toy. "Perhaps you had too much to drink the night before."

"I haven't drunk that much, not in a long, long time. But you're right, it was as though I had. So I went to wash my face, felt sick in my belly, but I couldn't focus. Every thought I had kept taking me downhill. And then, I began hearing this voice."

Jacob shifts as though he wants to be the one asking the questions, but he holds his peace as my mother continues. "What voice?"

"It was a woman's voice, but deep, sounded strange. Not quite old, but deep like that."

"I understand what you mean." It is the first I've spoken since the interrogation began. The man shakes his head slowly and then stares at me as though seeing me for the first time. "I didn't mean to hurt you. I know I did."

"Yes, well . . ."

"She made me do it," he whispers.

"She who?"

He turns to my mother again. "Her name is Ute—she said I must come down the mountain until I find you and take the young woman."

"What were you to do with Rapunzel?"

The frown that covers his face is rapid, his languid movements replaced now by panic. "Bring her to Ute."

"Where is Ute?"

"Up to her—I don't know where—just—I just know that is what she wanted from me." He is now struggling against his bonds, straining as though he must get free. "I need to do as she has said!"

"You can stop now. We won't let her hurt you."

"You can't stop me—I have to do what she wants!"

His wrists become raw and will be bleeding from the constant struggle if he continues.

Jacob steps forward, addressing Paul. "He'll harm himself if we don't stop him from coming after us."

"Stop him how?" My heart thuds like a hollow gong while the men speak, as though somehow I should be able to stop this conversation from progressing where I don't want it to go.

"If he can't walk, he can't follow."

"How can a man of God make such a statement?" My voice sounds bewildered as I stare at Jacob.

"There is a greater good that God wants us to serve. We must care for the people who will be lost to starvation without their leaders. Without the kings the people will perish, so we need to make certain we find Ute and that she does not stop us from finding her."

I look to Paul. What will he say? Paul seems lost, confused. "Surely we can leave him tied up with some food to eat and water to drink."

"I'll find a way to get free!" The man grunts, still straining. "If you don't want me following you, you will have to find a way to stop me." He is laughing now, nervous, afraid of the consequence of his confession even as he continues to chafe his own wrists. "I can't stop myself."

I think back to my own bondage to Edmund and the witch; everyone has a choice. "You have a choice," I state, "I know you do. You can choose to stop this, choose to stop letting her determine what you will do. Set your mind on something better, make the choice to be free."

"There is no freedom for me now that she has a hold of me."

"Who is she that she gets to determine your life? You can't let her take all you have—you must decide."

Jacob walks forward. "You cannot free yourself, but you can accept the forgiveness of Christ and be freed."

Everything comes back to Christ with Jacob and even my beloved. Should it? I wrestle inside myself, wondering if that is truly the way of things. Am I wrong for thinking it might not be so?

"Even if Christ did come to set me free, it is too late, I think. She has a hold of me and she will never give up."

"She is not greater than our Lord. Even the Evil One, whom she serves, is not as great as he. They are much smaller, but they seem great to us because we are afraid and cannot imagine how God can use such dark things to shine his light."

The man laughs even as the veins in his neck bulge from his effort to free himself.

"Drink this." Jacob offers the wine bladder to the man, and he stops long enough to drink deeply. As he is drinking, Jacob strikes him across the legs with his staff and the man screams out in agony. "If you will not choose to stop following us, I will help you."

THE VILLAGE

There is no sign that the man is able to follow us, though I've taken to glancing behind us. The men too are weary as we continue higher. The trees have become mostly pine, though there are still some maples with burning red leaves turning russet as the days grow colder.

It is afternoon when we walk into a hollow village. It looks as though it was burned out when the other town was. The smell of charred buildings stings our lungs as we walk around. We find a small woman who still lives in the area. She says the rest of the village has fled to King Onfroi, but evidently there weren't many to begin with. In her little voice, she offers us room in her home and boarding for our animals outside. There was little that wasn't burned up, but she says she can make do till winter is over and her daughter's family returns with help.

The woman's name is Cateline, and she provides us with a warm basin of water to wash our face and hands. She prepares us a hot meal of fresh pottage. I am so grateful for her kindness. Will she let us pay her for her hospitality? Probably not, since she has learned Paul is King Onfroi's son and will want to pay homage with her generosity. What would it be like to live all alone in such a drafty room after everyone else has died or abandoned you? I look at my mother and realize for the first time that she can be described as a widow. Of course, I knew this, but I never thought to name her that.

Over our meal, Jacob looks at us with frank honesty. "Paul has tried to prepare you for what is ahead, but I'm afraid you don't understand what is really coming."

An ominous thunderclap interrupts his cautious warning, but my mother laughs. "I suppose you are trying to scare us?"

Something about her sits well with him, and again his stoic face breaks into a smile. "I suppose so. I just worry you ladies won't know how to handle what we are coming to. I don't think it was—forgive me for speaking ill of him —wise of the king to send you on this mission. Surely Paul and I could defeat this sorceress on our own."

The widow might be hard of hearing, but she perks up when the word "sorceress" is spoken. "Are you speaking of the sorceress who has made the kings ill?"

"Yes."

"Aye, there are those who have had many visions of her. Our little village was quite a happy place here, but that was before."

"Before the dragon's fire?"

"Oh, it began before that. It was almost innocent in its way, or so we thought. Just idle superstition. There's been no sorcery in these mountains since the War of Sorcery, or so we thought. But we were wrong. First it was the children, seeing strange dreams of women cackling, and we all thought 'twas the way of things with little 'uns, you know how they gets scared, sometimes they do. But no, these little frights seemed to jump and hop, seemed to gallop, if you will, and we discovered to our dismay that she could find us in our beds, with our heads safe upon our pillows."

The old woman rubs her hands together and I notice that Amis's eyes light up. He has found a kindred story-teller and he longs to hear more. Jacob, of course, only longs to know what is at work here. Even now I can see that his mind is busy trying to discover the shape of the ill things ahead.

"It began at Mass one day—it was the time of harvest, and you know what a jolly time that can be." Her crisp smile bunches up the wrinkles around her eyes and mouth. "I always did like that the best." Her eyes mist over, remembering better times, but Jacob clears his throat, pulling the old woman back. "Aye me, how the mind does wander a bit when one has no reason to watch it. You are my first guests in ever so long. My granddaughter used to have me come join her for a meal now and again, and when the twins took to teething, I would hold them. 'Course, that was before . . ." Her eyes spill tears. "When our priest began questioning the dear little ones, it seems they had all seen the same woman on the same night. Brother Davide, such a good monk, black as midnight, like you"—she nodded at Jacob before rambling on—"and come all the way from the Eastern Ports years ago to serve us, he was sure that there was something strange at work. He'd seen things like this where he come from. He made certain to bless us and anoint the little ones, to keep them safe. But there were those among us that had betrayed us."

Paul sits forward, looking hard at the woman. "What do you mean?"

"I mean, they was doing things they ought not have, things would make the devil be glad."

Her odd speech seems more so by the whistling and

lisping her mouth makes since so many of her teeth are missing. "The priest caught three of them practicing sorcery, and he burned them. The one he didn't catch came back, burned down the church when some of our children was learning with the priest. That's when the dragon came. The wicked man locked the church up with them all inside before the dragon swooped out of the sky, lighting everything up. Only a few homes survived. Mine did because it was so close to the river. Those that lived left for the winter. They begged me to come, but I'm an old woman. I've never lived anywhere but here." She looks to Paul in reverence. Does she think because he is the son of a king he has the answers? Her faded blue eyes overflow with sorrow. I cannot imagine the horrors of that day or the days that have followed. Poor Paul! I wonder what it is like to have someone look at you in that way. He is just a man, and though I love him, I wonder if he is ready for the responsibility that now crouches at his door.

He clears his throat and looks at Jacob, then back at her, uncertainty present. "I am so sorry for all you lost. Have there been any further attacks?"

"Who is left to attack?"

"You must choose whether to stay or join your family for the winter. You could travel with us, but the going may be rough before we reach the valley and my father's castle. I wish we could take you to the Fisher King's hearth. It is much warmer there."

She surprises us with a laugh. "Ah, boy, I cannot leave this little cove. It has always been my home. I did not mean to burden you. Just thinking my worries aloud. If I do not make it till spring, it is as the Lord wills." The woman smiles, showing her few teeth. "We have some food set aside from harvest that was not burned up. I just wish I were hale and able to rebuild before my family returns."

Jacob takes over as Paul looks visibly shaken. "You are doing as you should. You have shown true hospitality as the Lord said to, even in the midst of your grief. The ones you have opened your home to are now going to help you. We will find the source of this evil, the sorceress, and we will make certain that she and her followers are stopped from causing further harm. You are strong or you would not have survived this long."

I am grateful for the words that Jacob uses to express himself, but I see that Paul looks away, his shoulders slumped. I can only assume it has something to do with being a leader, which I know nothing about.

I take a deep breath as we conclude our meal and the woman allows my mother and I to help her ready the family bed for all of us. Amis cleans up the meal without complaint, but I notice he doesn't hum at first. After he catches me frowning at him, he makes a face at me and begins to whistle as he continues caring for our needs and then those of the horses, whom he chooses to sleep with. Who knew he would make a model servant?

Paul asks for us to use the loft. I know it will be much colder than the family bed, but I go up with him without a word.

"I am sorry for the chill," he says as he wraps himself around me and I feel his heat become my own, "but I needed to be alone with you. I needed to listen to y—" But he can't quite say what he wants to say. He is more eloquent with his subjects and with others than with me. There is something between us, and I don't know what it is. I feel a bubble of panic try to rise. Why are we physically so close if we are going to be so far apart in thought? But I allow him to love me and I love him back, hoping he understands it will be all right. Somehow, we will get through this.

e've left behind Cateline and her sad village. When we stop for the evening, I can tell that Amis is about to begin asking questions. But I have my own question I have longed to ask. "How did you come to train Paul?" I inquire of Jacob.

The monk surprises me with a laugh. I think this is the first time he has fully smiled at me. "I will never forget when I first met Paul. He had been sent by his father to train at his uncle's kingdom."

"I was so young." Paul looks almost embarrassed, but he is laughing in his good-natured way.

"You were angry! You didn't think you needed the training that your father thought you did."

"That is true enough. I thought that if I was good at hunting I shouldn't need more than that." Paul turns to me with a mock whisper that can be heard above our fire's crackle. "And, Rapunzel, I wasn't that good at hunting. I didn't know that the hunters in my father's kingdom were letting me find things they themselves had quarried." He clears his throat and sits back. "I knew so little of how the kingdom worked and how spoiled I was by my position."

Jacob shakes his head after tearing off a piece of the dried fish. "You were not spoiled as most princes are—you were just naive and thought you understood enough. You didn't want the responsibility they were trying to prepare you for."

A dark look crosses my beloved's features, but it is a passing cloud and he smiles it away as though swatting off a mosquito. "Well, still, you were quite patient with me."

"I had little choice in the matter."

Both men laugh, remembering something, and I feel slighted that I can't join in the laughter, though I can't imagine why. I look around. My mother smiles at their laughter, while Amis is hard at work hard chewing his mouthful. I shake off my feeling and ask another question. "What happened?"

"Paul needed to be trained to bear arms, to be a proper knight. He was sent to the Fisher King to receive that training and to learn to conduct the affairs of court. Now, the latter I could not help him with, but instead of having him receive his training from the master-at-arms, who had enough to do, they sent him to me. I had just returned from a time of solitude, seeking God, and been told that there was a young whelp who needed training. So, he boarded with me."

"Isn't that unusual?"

"Quite, but the Fisher King had his reasons. Paul needed to become a man of honor, a man who could be trusted in all circumstances, and the Fisher King felt that his faith needed a bit of trying."

I turn to Paul. "Why is that?"

"Because of the way I had been brought up—" Paul halts and shakes his head.

Jacob holds up a hand to stop me from inquiring further. "There are some things that we can't change: who our parents are, the way they live—these things can make us a certain way. But it doesn't determine everything, and that was the year Paul decided what kind of man he wanted to be. By the following summer, the Fisher King was proud to announce that Paul would be his heir, and he spent every summer with us after that."

"Until I came after you." Paul hazards a glance my way.

My lips press into a smile, but I can't really feel it. Why was Paul not to become heir until he had spent time with a warrior monk? What had his father wanted for him that was different than what the Fisher King wanted? I feel as though each time I tug this string, more of the story unravels, and I don't really know where it will lead. I only know I am jerked to a stop whenever I chance to follow.

I see my mother's face watching mine, lit by the amber flames. I get up and move away as though to relieve myself. I don't want her to see my doubts.

⌒⌒⌒

"WAKE UP!" No one should be this happy come morning, but Amis is bright and cheerful every morning.

My mother rolls over with a shiver and a groan. She is more like me, sedate for a time until she has had a bite to eat. Actually, she is quite amusing to watch when Amis goes to give her some watered wine to drink. She snaps her head at his chipper voice and hisses. He always laughs.

"I think the descent into the valley will be a pleasant change," Jacob says around a mouthful of dry bread.

"I think fresh provisions are in order." Paul nods. "We may not be able to expect much more than that."

Coming up the mountain, we see the road crossing through a meadow, a small valley of sorts with a clump of houses grouped together nearby. Paul has said that his father's kingdom is between this mountain and the next, and I wonder how much bigger the valley is that houses it. Would this village be a part of his kingdom, or would it be part of someone else's? I can't really understand what belongs to whom. Even as we travel, the map in my mind stretches and the borders and boundaries are a tangled mess of hazy lines.

I look into the meadow as I hear the bleating of goats and the sharp plunking of bells that are tied to a few of the throats. Goats are funny-looking creatures. They aren't soft and fluffy like the winter-ready sheep we have seen. These creatures are wiry, tough looking, with pointy little horns and obnoxious-sounding bleats. Their rambunctious tempers cause them to run up and butt things, but seeing them makes me hopeful. I remember what my mother said about growing up with goats and what they sold in town.

There should be milk and cheese here! I feel as though my stomach hasn't had anything fine to eat in ever so long. I am that grateful to see the houses ahead. The boy out in the meadow dashes to us with a wide smile. As many people in the mountains are, he is fair-skinned, and his thick hair is combed back into a tight braid. "Welcome to our meadow. My name is Piers. Have you need of a place to stay?"

I can't help the laugh that bubbles up from inside me as Paul helps me dismount. "What a wonderful welcome. Yes, we do. We have been on this journey for such a long time."

"Where are you going?"

"We are traveling to King Onfroi's kingdom."

"You have only another day's ride ahead of you—but please first, stay the night at my father's hearth. I know that he will welcome you as I have. We have the best cheese and the best bread. My mother will be happy to feed you. We will give you our bed for the night, and longer if you wish to stay."

How incredibly generous! He leads us toward the first thatch-roofed dwelling we come to. An apple-cheeked woman greets us at the door as the boy leads our horses away to the town stable. She is tall, as these Northlanders seem to be, with their narrow shoulders. I see by her smile the dimpled resemblance between mother and son.

"Come in, come in!" she greets us, as she wipes her hands on the apron she has tied over her surcoat. She fairly pushes us inside a wide cabin that is partitioned into an eating area and a sleeping area. I have to watch where I step, as both areas are speckled with chickens underfoot. "Supper is nearly ready, and I made enough for guests. I—I often make more than we can eat, we are only too happy to share. My husband should be in soon with my older son. He went to the smithy this evening while our youngest son was caring for the goats. Of course, you saw that our son was caring for the goats, I suppose that's how he met you! Do you like goat cheese? Here, have some!" She begins shoving us on the hard benches. "You must eat, it is the best in the meadow, everyone says."

The strong cheese is soft and melts in my mouth. She sloshes a jug of something with a frothy head onto the table, but it doesn't smell like ale. I breathe in the scent, which reminds me of cloves. "You must try our mead. We have our own bees and make ever so much. You will have to take some with you to wherever you are going."

"Thank you for taking us in." But the words come out

sounding strange to me, as though I am not the one speaking, but it is somebody else.

"It is our duty and honor to open our home to anyone who comes through here." Her intense stare leaves me uneasy. "We have been waiting for you."

"Waiting for us?"

"Yes, of course—she said you would be coming."

"Wait, who said we would be coming?"

"The woman, she was tall and said that behind her there were travelers coming this way and we should be prepared to receive them."

I glance at Paul, whose brow is furrowed. Amis is sitting on the bench next to Paul, his face darkened in concern. There is something at work here, but I'm not sure what it is. I can sense something wrong, leaving a sour tang in my mouth. I stare at the woman and notice the shimmer.

She begins laughing. "You are getting closer, aren't you, dear Rapunzel? I'm glad of it!" Her laughter is disturbing, her voice no longer that of the woman who greeted us. It is that deep, velvety tone that haunts my dreams.

As though she can hear my thoughts, she shakes her head. "Don't suppose you can understand what I am about. Only know that the completion of what I have planned will bring together my sisters. No longer will we be bound to the land or the sea that separates us. We can be together once more, and never again will a man rule over us, commanding that women die when it suits him."

What is she talking about?

"I know what you men are like." She has turned on Paul. "You think you can make the decisions for all of us women, but you can't. You'll find your decisions weak and unwanted. We will rise, we will leave your 'protection.' We don't need you!"

The woman laughs once more and then she shivers; the glimmer fades, and she sways as though dizzy. Paul is up and catching her before she falls to the floor.

A man is standing in the doorway, but I don't know how long he has been there. His head leans sideways as though listening to something from far away. His deep melodic voice begins to sing, travelling up and travelling down like a staircase that never leads anywhere. The words are strange and I can't quite understand them. They are in that language I don't know, though I have heard it before. The witch sometimes sang in it, and I can hear Ute in him now. Perhaps I've even heard this very song. But what does it mean?

"Don't you know, Rapunzel, don't you remember? You will never be safe in their world—you must come to mine." Her voice comes out of the man and then he hacks up a cough. He wobbles and tries not to fall over as she leaves him. He becomes himself again, or as much himself as he can be, having been possessed so recently.

You might think that supping with people just possessed by a sorceress would be strange—and indeed, you would be correct. We take our meal in embarrassed silence. The couple and their sons seem afraid for what they have experienced, afraid at having to share a meal and their home with people who have been targeted by the sorceress. We are ashamed that we have brought this kind of danger to this family, into their beloved home. They are quiet, as anyone might be, and I wonder how many more polite nothings we can say. We finally all go to bed, but I don't think anyone actually rests.

THE MOUNTAIN KING

$\mathcal{A}$pproaching a castle from above seems a strange thing. Most fortresses are up on a hill, sometimes surrounded by a moat. This one is not. Instead, it is deep inside the valley with the Ventrias cutting in front of it and the mountain's edge behind it. Enemies would have to clamber down the mountain to come in from behind or find a way to cross the river without the drawbridge lowered.

As we enter, an attendant runs over to us and helps us with the horses. As we get down, I stare up at the ornate staircase that leads to the entrance of the castle. On either side of the doors are two attendants dressed in the dark green that Paul used to wear when we first met. I had noticed this morning that he was wearing it again, and I asked if it was to meet his father. He said yes, though he didn't know when we would actually receive an audience with the king.

"He hasn't seen you in over a year! How could he not want to see his own son right away?"

"Because he is my father, and he won't want to see us

until it suits him." Paul's jaw was clenched, and it seemed as though he wanted to say something else, but Jacob shook his head. That's all it took: a simple shake of Jacob's head, and my husband stopped talking to me.

The silence between us was thick as we rode out.

Paul is greeted warmly by a steward, but he is told that the king is busy. Paul gives me a knowing look as we are each taken to our chambers. Brother Jacob and Amis disappear with their servant escorts, and my mother is taken to the guest wing. Paul and I are escorted to his bedchambers when he explains that we are married. I notice that the servant smiles on hearing the news, but says nothing. It is a sedate, grey-stoned castle. Though many people are running about, quite busy, each one is quiet and has a tense expression etched across their face. What on earth could have put such a look there?

Paul's bedchamber is lovely. The mahogany bed is adorned with dark-green velvet curtains, blankets, and cushions. The servant who brings us inside gestures to the washbasin that has just been filled. "We will bring a tub for you to bathe in." He says this without asking what we want before shutting the door.

"I suppose that means we stink." Paul laughs. "It is best that we bathe before my father sees us. He is quite fastidious about these things."

I join his laughter, relieved to see him smile. "I suppose that made your childhood difficult. From the little I know of small boys, they love to run and get dirty."

"Yes, he always wanted me to clean up and be presentable by mealtime, or when there was another nobleman around. You have to understand—the springs in this valley and up higher in the mountains are supposed to heal people. People come from all over the Northlands and beyond for their chance to soak in them. My brother and I were trained to look and sound the way my father wanted so we didn't embarrass him. My brother was always good at that sort of thing."

"But not you?"

He shakes his head. "I have not the same way with people like my brother. He can put others at ease. As the next in line for the throne, he's always been expected to." He stops short when the servants arrive with our tub and several pitchers of heated water. "You first." He motions to the tub.

My shyness returns in the light of day, so I go behind a screen to undress as he continues talking. "The summer I met you, I was surprised when he allowed me to take my brother's place at the High King's court."

"What do you mean?"

"Nothing. Umm—the servant is here for you. I'll leave you to your bath." I come out wearing a robe that was hooked to the screen. I'm more than uncomfortable. He must sense this, but laughs again. "It's going to be fine, Rapunzel, you don't have to let them bathe you. I won't let anyone do it for me either, not since I was much younger. My father will just have to accept us for who we are, or not at all." Paul kisses me lightly on the temple. "You wore a green gown the day we were wed, yes?"

I remember the morning I couldn't sleep and got dressed in the dark to go poke around the Fisher King's castle. I had been happy to have found my favorite gown, not knowing I would be wearing it to my own wedding that night. Was that only a month ago? I hadn't known then it would be the last time in a long while that I would wear a normal dress. "Yes, I still have it," I answer.

"Wear that for now, and we will be provided with more if we stay longer. When you are queen, you may wear the blue of the Fisher King's realm. Until then, you are the wife of the Prince of the Soontrisse Mountains. Remember, it is best to stay on his good side when we can, which may not be often." He smiles while he says all of this. I can't understand why it would make him smile. Expressions at times like this are often alien to me.

Paul lets himself out, and after accepting the lavender soap and other necessary bathing items, I shoo out the remaining servants and get to work. The sigh that escapes my lips as I sink into the tub is long and low. My mind drifts as I allow the water to pull me in.

At last I notice that the water has cooled and I make myself get out. If I had let a servant wait on me, they would have refreshed the water so I could stay longer, but, no matter. I really should get out and let Paul have some time to relax.

It takes only a moment to dry off and don my familiar layers of dress: the chemise, then cotehardie, and finally the sideless surcoat embroidered with silk leaves. But it feels strange not to wear hosen! And the seams in the dresses— why do they feel so tight? I suppose my riding clothes have changed how these once-familiar clothes now feel.

I brush back my hair, knowing I will have to ask for help to make it look acceptable for the king's presence. My hair is not long enough to split down the middle, braid, and coil above my ears. Nervous laughter bursts out; I could try it, but they would make absurdly small buns. Will my feet and lack of ettiquette trip over unknown rules?

All I know of high society has taught me that each land has its own way of doing things, and I know so little of the Northlands. The Fisher King made me welcome in his kingdom, but if Paul doesn't feel at home here, how will I? Why won't Paul tell me more of his life so that I won't embarrass him before his father? I wish I understood the way his mind worked. I feel as though I don't know which way to step.

⁂

THIS IS AWKWARD, I think to myself as we sit down at last in the king's bedchamber. He, like the Fisher King, is drawn and pale beneath his cap. His cheekbones are sharp and his cheeks are hollow. How hard it must be to give him a close shave! He sits propped up by cushions, but still sinks into them. Sitting at the king's left hand, Queen Gila wears the same dark green as the bedding. Paul's brother's wife, Aalis, stands nearby next to ornate chairs. Though pale and uncomfortable, she declines to sit as long as we are standing. We shift and glance about. No one here knows what to say.

Paul at last breaks through the silence. "Father, I would like to introduce to you Rapunzel, my bride, and her mother, Katterina." We both bow into deep curtsies of respect. I lower my eyes as I should, but not before noticing that all three of these royal personages are staring at me as though I am a peculiar bird, something exotic and strange. Paul launches into the story of our meeting, but his father is quick to hold up a trembling hand. "I am sure that you first went to see your uncle before coming here."

"I did."

"And he knows of your bride?"

"We were married at his hearth."

"Then we are glad that he approves your choice." I suppose what crosses his face could be termed a smile, but I am hard-pressed to call it that. "What concerns us now is why you have come here."

"I have heard of the illness that the kings of the Northlands are all suffering from. My uncle is not well." I notice Paul says nothing about his father's illness.

King Onfroi nods. "Yes, it is bad, but as you can see, we are still well enough to receive you, and we will soon return to good health."

Paul nods a little too quickly. "I'm sure you will."

"We are still able to rule, and while we have been ill your brother has been of the utmost help to us."

I look again at the still form of the queen. Her face is blank. Is she even aware we are here? She shows no emotion about seeing her long-absent son and doesn't act disturbed by her husband's rapidly declining health. Nothing. Her hair is prematurely white, with a few streaks of the brown I see in Paul's hair. Her eyes are hazel like his, but other than that, there is nothing about her that seems like him. She is sitting tall and stiff, unmoving. Paul said she was a different woman, happy and able to laugh aloud in the Fisher King's castle. I try to imagine her happy there, but I can't.

Paul's brother, Prince Roland, bursts into the room. He is not at all what I expected. A large man with great girth, he rushes over to Paul and hugs him tightly. "Oh, brother, it is that good to see you again! We had nearly given up all hope, hadn't we, Father?"

"We wouldn't state it quite that way."

"Wouldn't you, though? Of course you would. We thought you were lost and—oh! I see you have brought a maid. Who is she?"

"She is Rapunzel, and she has become my wife in the Fisher King's court."

"Has she, indeed? Wonderful, wonderful! It is time we have received some good news! We have need of it just now. Come, you must tell us all about your adventures and wooing this young woman to your side."

Paul is unsurprised by his garrulous brother. His shoulders lower from their stiff position and he leans forward as though to relate our strange tale.

"There's time enough for that later," barks the hoarse king as he tries to resume control of his sick-chamber. "We have much more serious things to discuss and we cannot be distracted by a mere marriage.

"Now, Paul, why are you here instead of with the Fisher King?"

"As I have said, he is unwell, Your Majesty." Paul concedes. "But when we met with him, he sent us to go find the source of this curse. The monk who has traveled with us is the same one that I trained with at the Fisher King's court so long ago."

At this, Queen Gila's face twitches.

"In fact, please send for him now. Even if he is at prayer, he will come. He knows how vital it is for Your Majesty to understand what we have ascertained about this troubling ill health in the Northland kings."

It is not long before a servant returns with Brother Jacob, who bows and waits quietly, his hands tucked within his sleeves like a muff. I notice that he looks at Her Majesty with something beyond curiosity, but when she glances up, he quickly looks away. Her frown appears as Jacob addresses the king. "How can I serve you, Your Majesty?"

"We need to understand why the Fisher King has sent such a strange group to discover the problems surrounding this illness."

"Surely your son has related some of the tale to you by now."

"We would like to hear it from you, a man of God."

At this the monk frowns. "The Fisher King believes with me that this curse that has infected the kings of the Northlands is caused by Ute."

"The grand sorcerer's eldest daughter?"

"She is bound to these mountains, is she not?"

"Well, yes, but why would she be causing mischief after all this time?"

"We believe that another witch, a pupil of hers, spent the past two decades preparing to reunite the sisters. This spell and illness is now a culmination of that plan."

The queen leans over to straighten the bedsheets, but the king waves her away. "How do you know these things for certain?"

"I have spent a great deal of time in prayer and searching out what God's will is. When Rapunzel and her mother came to the Fisher King and I heard their story, I knew that they were part of this greater puzzle."

The king's eyes narrow as he now turns to my mother. "Explain to me how."

"My sister was Eufemia, the witch who was Ute's pupil . . ." my mother begins. I aid in telling the tale, misgiving heavy on me as the king furrows his brow.

"This is outrageous!" The king tries to bellow at last, but it comes out a strained whisper. "Paul, you have married the spawn of a witch?"

His mother has stopped her fidgeting, and her eyes look as though they will overflow. *What have I done to my beloved? Will our union forever separate him from his family?*

"No, father, she is not the child of a witch—"

Jacob intervenes, holding up a hand of peace. "Even if she were, it would not be her burden, sire. The sins of the mother will not be reckoned on the child anymore. It states this very clearly in scripture."

"Does it?" The queen's voice shocks me. She has said nothing in all this time, and she looks on the monk as though he has changed everything with this one proclamation.

"No." His baritone voice lowers. "I thought so at one time, but I was wrong. It is clear to me now that Christ came to set people free from all sin, and that when forgiveness is accepted, it can free one even from the sins passed down from parent to child."

Queen Gila's face crumples and she runs out of the room. The king looks bewildered and sends an attendant after her. No one says anything more of her sudden departure, though she didn't seem the high-strung type to me.

"Somehow, we must make sense of what is going on, Father." Paul's brother looks as though he wishes he could somehow make us each quiet down, settle things amicably. But how can he? The king has insulted me, and though I have been insulted before, I doubt Paul is going to let it stand. I'm confused, baffled by this turn of events. There is an undercurrent flowing beneath the words of each person who speaks. A glance sent my mother's way shows she is watching, her eyes unblinking. As usual, she is taking in each bit of information. What is she seeing that I am not?

"We will leave at once!" I have never seen Paul so furious, but his father holds up that same trembling hand. Paul halts. "You will not leave unless we tell you to. You will go ready yourself for the meal, and we will discuss this more, later." The king's face is pinched, drained of all blood. He must be exhausted by the fury that settled over him when he realized who I was and what I was bringing into his family.

Paul shocks me. Instead of taking me and departing as he said he would, his shoulders round and he seems to shrink. We retreat to his bedchambers and wait to be called to sup with the king in the evening.

BROTHERS

I stare at my husband as he paces while I sit on the bed watching. Who is this? When did he become so indecisive? His face is a tight mask that refuses to speak, but I must know what all this is about. Just as I am about to ask, there is a knock on the large door.

"Come in!" Paul huffs.

There stands Prince Roland, his belly dipping the belt of his tunic down like an upside-down frown. "Paul, you must understand—"

"What must I understand? That our father is unreasonable? He told me long ago that it mattered not to him who I married. Even when I first came here, he did not care."

"He didn't think you'd bring a witch's child into his kingdom. He didn't think you'd bring in a—a transformed cat. You know that he—"

"There is no reason it should concern him! I am not his heir, and he need not see me again except in the High King's hall."

"Perhaps you think not, but you will be his heir after all."

"What?"

"Princess Aalis cannot give me another child—at least she has not been able to yet." He shrugs with a sad smile. "After we lost Enguerrand, it devastated Aalis. We looked everywhere—"

"Wait, what?"

"We searched everywhere, but we never found trace of the nursemaid or our baby boy."

"I thought you lost him, that he died right after childbirth."

"No, we lost him because he was stolen. It nearly broke us. Well, it did break Aalis. She has miscarried twice since then. She now rarely leaves our chambers. I know I should put her away and take a mistress, but I have grown to love her. I cannot abandon her like so many kings are wont to do."

"Our uncle could not act that way, either."

Roland shifts his stance. "No, but our father does not understand my hesitation. He cannot abide that in this thing I will not do as he wishes."

"Surely he still wants the alliance with her father to remain strong?"

"Oh, of course he does, but he doesn't think that my taking a mistress will cause any problems with her family." He grimaces. "You remember what her father was like with his mother."

"Not always the same thing as having someone else cast aside your daughter." Paul sounds bitter. Caustic?

I feel as though I should leave. I know they are discussing me and yet not discussing me. My eyes drift to the floor as Paul continues his questions. "What can be done?"

The sad but smiling brother walks over to a beautiful carved chair against the wall and sits down with a whoosh.

"If I'm not able to produce an heir before our father dies, he has told me in no uncertain terms that he will leave the kingdom to you."

"He can't do that!" Paul spouts.

"He can and he will. He thinks that he can change my mind, but I don't have to have the kingdom to be happy. I know very well you can combine the mountains and the Fisher's Kingdom into a formidable force. I would only be too happy to act as your steward and do as you wish when you weren't here to oversee things."

Paul looks torn between anger and astonishment. His energy forces him to pace in frustration. "He can't do that to you! He's never even liked me. You've always been the son he wanted, the one that would give him everything. He was proud of your training, your marriage alliance, your schooling. My whole life he has been disappointed in how I kept to myself, how I loved the hunt but couldn't sit through long lessons. He said it was just as well the Fisher King had me because he didn't know what to do with me."

"He may have said all those things, but he has always been proud of you."

Paul chokes on a laugh.

"It's true! Anytime you weren't around, I saw how he admired your fortitude, how he liked your ability to know what you wanted from life. It angered him to give you over to the Fisher King, but if he didn't, our uncle would have cut off the trade through the port."

"None of this can be true. You must be speaking of a different man. Our father has always disapproved of me."

Roland is shaking his head with a sorrowful smile. "No, brother, it has always been you who has been disappointed in him."

The room is silent. There is nothing, no intake of

breath, no movement as we each absorb what has just been said.

"He was never a good father to us and has always been a horrible husband. He knows you to be a man of integrity. You grate on him."

"Why me and not you?" Paul walks over to the bedside table and pours a drink, shaking his head.

"I was the heir, so I went along with things that you never would. He cannot abide that."

"What will he do now?"

"I don't know—but I do know that if you are to go, then you must go now. Don't wait for another meal, don't wait for another word. He will only slow you down on your mission. You can't please him. I have tried longer and harder than you, and it is no use. Look at our mother—she gave everything she has ever had, and it has given her precious little. I think the saddest day of her life was the day that our grandfather told her she would have to marry our father. Don't you think she would have been happier to have never married at all?" He shrugs; it's a question neither son can answer. "You can leave, so do it. Complete your mission for the king who has always wanted you. If our father wants you for an heir, he will choose to do so, and I will serve you faithfully." He walks over to Paul and puts his hands on his shoulders.

Paul blinks hard and clears his throat. "Brother, I pray God will grant you many children to fill your home."

"Aye, may he do so and help my wife dry her eyes." The two brothers embrace, putting aside any enmity that tried to come between them from their father's mishandling.

"Are you heading to the peak?"

"Yes."

"Then beware the stories we were told as children. I no

longer think the tales of the enchanted castle and dragon are fanciful tales to get little ones to sleep."

"We will be careful."

"Be quick about it, then—you know how difficult it will be to get there."

"I do."

THE HUNT

The air crackles with frustration and anger, but I don't know how to soothe my husband's scowl, I don't know how to relax his raised shoulders. Before we leave his room, Paul asks a servant to gather our group together in the inner bailey in order to leave. I notice a bow and arrow hanging on the wall. "Is that yours?"

"One of mine, yes. The one I liked best of all was lost when I was thrown from your tower."

I take a deep breath. I don't think he meant to sound as though he blamed me for the loss of the bow. Still . . . "You learned to hunt here, didn't you?"

"I did." A quirk plays around the edges of his mouth. "I can show you where."

"Don't just show me where, show me how." I wrap myself once more in my warm green cloak.

"What?"

"I want to see you hunt, I want to see what you are like when you are hunting. I think it's been too long for you."

"I haven't hunted since Rona. You can't call fishing off the side of the ship hunting."

"No, I don't suppose you can."

He smiles as he takes the bow and arrow from the room, moving past the servants gathering our things. When we mount in the inner bailey, the smile is still on his face. Paul relates the new plan to the group, and Jacob smiles at his confidence. Rather than leaving the valley directly and heading up into the mountains, we make camp in a lovely wood where I assume many of the people hunt to supplement their meals.

Heading into the wood is wondrous. I feel at home once we are here. There is a word in the Allerian language meaning *to be at one with the trees*, and that word makes me feel like I belong. I want to always live near trees. The colors of autumn are falling fast as the wind blows, scenting the air with a loamy fragrance. I am amazed at how even these fading colors always fill me with joy. For a moment, I am happy. There are no witches or sorceresses predetermining what we should or should not do. Things said in anger and frustration drift away. Like a deep sigh returning breath to the body, our group relaxes as we make camp.

The following morning, Amis, Jacob, and my mother have a day of rest, while Paul shows me what prints to look for. We creep through the wood, looking for deer. He remembers where in the wood they like to eat and other details concerning their habits. With gestures, he instructs me as to how to act as we wait. I can't help but notice that his shoulders have dropped. I risk a quiet whisper. "Was it here that you caught sight of the mist that led you to me?"

His laugh is quiet, his voice low. "It was an ordinary morning, and it had been such a long while since I had scouted new territory. I needed to relieve boredom, not an aching belly, so I had the time and leisure to go and look. This valley is large, but I had scouted much of it—which is why, when I caught a glimpse of sunflowers, I knew some-thing was wrong, something was different."

"Do you think it was magic?" I have contemplated this for far too long. I must give voice to my fears and doubts.

"No, I think it was God."

I feel a frown pucker my brow. "I thought maybe my witch let you see the sunflowers and allowed you to come to me to test me."

"No, I think it was the way that God wanted to release you and free me."

"Free you?"

"Rapunzel, you were not the only prisoner——"

But he won't elaborate just now—a buck has come into the area. I can count the sharp white points of his antlers. His huge brown eyes scan the trees, but we are still clothed in the dark greens of the kingdom. Though there are many red and orange leaves that have fallen, the colors are now muted. The brown tree trunks, green bushes, and ferns mask us where we crouch. Paul lifts the bow and notches an arrow to the string. He pulls back and lets fly. The sound of the wounded deer pierces me as it thuds to the ground in a great heap.

"Paul! It's hurt!"

"Of course it's hurt." He laughs. "That was the whole point." Without saying anything more, he jumps to his feet and runs over to the wounded animal, slitting its throat so it bleeds out crimson blood on the brown leaves.

"I'm sorry," I mumble, "I didn't want it to suffer."

"Nor did I." His face is flush.

He waits until it bleeds out and then puts the buck up over his shoulders and walks us back to camp.

◌⁀◌

OUR FOOD IS delicious and I find my heart swelling with pride. I know that in the Fisher King's realm we will eat many fish, but I must make certain that Paul has a chance to hunt as often as possible. I've never seen him quite this happy, at least not since we were first wed.

"I know we need to continue on tomorrow, but I'm glad we did this." Paul leans back onto his elbows, his feet toward the fire. The bright flames pop and hiss as they consume the branch's sap.

My mother looks at me and smiles. It crosses my mind to wonder how she is doing on this arduous journey. I know that she wandered without a home for twenty years; surely she is tired of this life and longs for a place to settle.

Amis laughs. "You know, there was a man I met one day that this reminds me of."

"What reminds you?"

"This meal. I always did like venison, and I have heard that when Paul would come to the castle and lead a hunt there would be venison for weeks. Is it true?"

Jacob nods, his dark, thick lips stretching into a near-smile. "The Fisher King was always happy to share his wood with Paul."

"I would think too many fish might weary some after a while." Amis widens his eyes knowingly at me, and I laugh without meaning to. This strange jester, always knowing what is on my mind!

"We're lucky to have meat so often. When I was a child, we only had meat on Sundays," Jacob says between bites.

"Indeed, meat on Sundays would give you something to get through Mass for—no offense, Brother Jacob. There is many a dreary Sunday that I have worried about such things, you know."

Jacob coughs as though to nudge Amis forward. "You were going to tell us a story."

"Now, was I?"

"No more chasing about, Amis, either tell the story, or give us a rest and let's enjoy the harmony of the fire."

"I wouldn't want to deprive you of such a pleasure, but perhaps once you've heard my story you will enjoy the fire that much more. It begins late one night when an old man and an old woman realize they have little left to eat in their home. The old man had been a cobbler, but his shop had fallen on hard times. A drought of sorts had settled on the land, and most of the people had given up wearing shoes. They just couldn't afford such finery. Not that a great many of them wore shoes anyway, but those that did gave them up."

Amis lets his gaze drift over the flames before he begins to speak again. "So the old man wakes up one morning and he tells his wife that he's going hunting. The wife nods her head and bites her cheek to not laugh. The reason the old man was a cobbler was because he couldn't hunt at all, not even to supplement their meals when the children were young." Amis knowingly points his chin at Paul and I. "Sometimes growing children need more food than you'd expect. So the old man gets up early that next morning and he toddles out to the woods.

"Of course, he is so loud he can't catch a deer, but one of his traps lands a rabbit before the day is over. The old man returns triumphant and the old woman is singing his praises as she skins and cooks the hare.

"Just as they are sitting down to thank God for the meal, there comes a knock at their door. The man opens up to find a small family of a young man, his wife, and their small child. They haven't eaten in days, and though the old man and his wife had thought to stretch the rabbit stew over the coming days, they know they have to share. They give large portions to the young parents and child. When evening darkens the sky, they also give their bed to the young family. When the dawn colors the following morning with streaks of pink and orange, the old woman takes the last of their bread and shares it for breakfast before the family leaves.

"The old couple have nothing left to eat after that, so the old man goes once more to check on his traps in the wood. He is still too loud to get a deer, but he is able to easily find another rabbit, though this one is smaller than the first. But it will make a good meal, and he is only too happy to bring it home to his wife. When she roasts it, the entire home smells of heaven and their mouths began to water. They have not eaten since the stew, but just as they sit down, yet another knock cames on the door.

"This time, there is a priest standing outside, much like yourself, Jacob. He needs a place to stay and a meal to eat. With no thought for themselves, they invite him in. They share a large portion of the rabbit and then offer him their bed. He does not stay to dine the next morning. He tells them that he has to move on and will get something for himself on his way. The old man tries not to pity himself, but returns to the wood.

"This time, the rabbit trap is bare. His face is drawn on his return, and his wife holds out her arms to him. 'We once had plenty, but now we have nothing. Still, our life together has been good, old man. I would not change a bit of it.' 'Not even for the best hunter?' he asks in a mournful tone. 'No,' she says, and as she bends to kiss him, a knock on the door comes.

"When the old man opens the door, he shakes his head sadly at the man who stands there. 'I'm sorry to say we have no food to share, but if you have a need to lay your head down, you can certainly rest here.' As soon as he has spoken thus, the young man disappears and a mighty man in shining garments stands before them, holding a sword. 'You have shared when you had so little. Did you not know that you were sharing with messengers from God himself?'

"The news stuns the old man and his wife—they can't believe what is being said to them! One by one, the visitors from the past few days reappear and come through their door. They are shining with bright light so that the couple has to shield their eyes. 'This is too great for me!' The old man cries. But the heavenly visitors remind him that what he did for the least was, in fact, serving the Son of God. And so, the old man and old woman were provided for with food till the end of their days."

It is quiet after Amis stops his tale, and none of us speaks. I think of my meager abilities, the little that I can accomplish. If I decide to trust in this God, will what I give him be enough?

POSSESSION

Our morning ride has taken us up past the valley where the trees are thinning. I can see out below us, and for once it doesn't make me feel as though I'm—

Something comes flashing past us and goes over the side of the mountain, a blur of color in motion and a sickening thud. A sound of wailing echoes from high up above with a chorus of goats bleating. Paul is off his horse faster than I can think, looking down below.

"Help me!" His uncertainty evaporates in the face of urgency.

Jacob is by his side, acting as a belay after the rope is anchored. Slowly, slowly the rope is let out, until Paul has his feet on the ledge. He secures the rope around a lump of a woman, and Jacob and Amis pull her to safety. My mother is fast to get on her knees and check the woman.

The poor thing's face is scratched on one cheek and bleeding; a pool of blood seeps through her hair from the wound on her head. Her body looks broken. I don't know what we can do. Certainly we can't do anything here on this narrow trail. When Paul is back up from the ledge, the men help ready her and put her on Paul's horse. We continue up the mountain, toward whoever it is that we can hear crying and moaning.

We make our way into a small village where a crying girl is surrounded by bleating goats in a patch of grass The village is tiny, with only a few houses lined up, their backs made of the mountain's side. I see no places to board animals and no ale house.

The woman isn't breathing properly as Jacob lowers her to the ground. Taking her hands in his hands in his, he intercedes. "God, hear our prayer, please relieve this woman of the pain she is in. Heal her broken body, Lord, for her wounds are more than we can fix—"

A group gathers, including a tall, muscular man who swoops the moaning little girl into his arms. Her father, perhaps? But the child won't have it and pushes out of his arms. She pushes her small frame through the crowd, singling out a woman with wild eyes. Her voice is screaming as she points with slobbery fingers she was sucking on. "You pushed! You pushed!"

The father turns toward the red-headed woman. "What did you do?"

"I didn't do anything!" The woman holds her hands out in front of her, shaking her head vigorously.

"You pushed! You pushed!" the child cries, pummeling her little fists against the thighs of the woman.

"I didn't—I didn't mean to!"

"What happened?" barks the man, advancing.

"It wasn't me, it was someone else, something else. I was standing there, watching the goats and talking and— my hands—"

"What did you do?" He yanks the woman by her red hair and yells into her face.

"I don't know! I just—"

"You pushed! You pushed!"

The woman blubbers, her neck craned, face red as her hair and slick with tears.

"Look at your sister—she won't last the night!"

At our feet, the woman's strangled breath is faint, and I look at the one accused of pushing her. Her face is creased with confusion; her eyes are spilling out tears of regret. "I don't know what happened!"

"You pushed Mama!"

"No! Just—the wind was blowing and the goats got angry and—"

"The goats what?"

"They growled. I was scared, I ran away, I went to the path and she ran after me shouting in some strange tongue and I—I don't know! I turned around and—it wasn't me! I was someone else, but my body lunged at her, pushed her over the edge. I was shrieking, screaming, I don't know what's wrong with me!"

I want to be sick, but there are people pressing in all around us. The crowd is now roaring for her to pay, to pay for what she has done. "But I didn't mean to! I don't know what happened! Please—please!"

They grab her and push her to the ground. She hits it hard, and feet stomp on her, kicking her in the side, in the head. She pulls her knees into her body and covers her face with her hands. "Kill her! Kill her!" The husband is frothing at the mouth, his voice an incomprehensible growl. The people are screaming, hissing like angry cats in heat.

"No!" my mother shouts, running to cover the woman with her own body. But these aren't people— these are angry animals who can't think. Paul and Amis try to intercede, but before they can, Jacob steps forward with his staff and swipes at the husband who is now kicking my mother. The man turns his rage on Jacob. With both hands, Jacob lunges forward and sweeps the staff, hitting the man's shoulder, missing his head. The man is quick and takes the blow. He counter-lunges and tries to take the staff, but Jacob is too swift. He backs away, spinning and using the momentum to whack the side of the man's face. The blow should knock the man to the ground, but the man smiles. He laughs—and it is then that I hear it. It's not him laughing, it's *her*. How is she possessing them? How is she going from being to being?

"Jacob!" I cry, unsure if he can understand me while fighting. "Ute is using him."

"Get out in the name of Jesu!" The monk holds the staff horizontally and thrusts it up under the man's throat, pushing up and propelling the man back. While the man is trying to breathe and regain his footing, Jacob jerks backward. He spins the staff and uses it like a club, driving the end into the man's chest. This time the man crumbles to the ground, and the crowd falls back as the man wheezes for air. His eyes roll back into his head and shut.

Jacob kneels down beside my mother and lifts her off the wounded woman. How hurt is she?

"It was Ute!" I gasp, still reeling that she is continuing to attack us, now stronger than ever.

"Of course it was," Jacob says and looks at Paul. "We should have expected this. Any time an enemy is threatened—"

"They will redouble their efforts to stave off the attack —to reroute the enemy. She is doing everything she can to keep us from coming to destroy her."

No. She is drawing us in—I feel it deep within me. Somehow, this is what she is doing, pulling us forward, and she knows this will only induce us to keep coming, convince ourselves we are doing the right thing, that we must continue.

Jacob tends to the sisters but shakes his head over them. There is nothing to be done. Both the women lie together, their breaths shallow and now slowing. The child weeps into her mother's hair for a time. When she raises her head, she glares with ferocity at her aunt. She's too young to grasp that the woman was controlled by a sorceress. I wonder if she will ever be able to care for her goats again without the nightmares that will come. I fear for her nightmares; I hope she is spared them. Perhaps no one else is visited like I am in the night.

⌒⊂⊃⌒

JACOB KNEELS for a long while beside my mother before we take our evening meal in the home that has been lent to us. No one would dare take us into their home, but there is a house that was abandoned a few winters ago when an older couple died. We are allowed this deserted place, and here we rest, trying to recover. We have been told in clear terms that we are not welcome in their church and that we must move on as soon as my mother is able to leave.

She is weak now, having sprinted into danger to cover that woman with her own body. I didn't know she would take the blows of another, act as a shield. Why have I not seen this about her before? I should have known it from the way she has cared for me during this trip. For now, my anger is laid to rest as I watch her struggle.

Jacob and Paul say to forgive, and I know they are right, but how does one do that over and over again? Forgiveness should flow from the heart, shouldn't it? Sorrow fills me at the sight of her mottled, black-and-purple face.

A quiet prayer comes from Jacob, and something in his demeanor causes me to pause. What are the feelings between them? The way she looks up at him, how he looks down at her, his tone as he whispers her name . . . He turns when he realizes they are not alone and he coughs a bit, slipping his hand out of hers.

"I think Katterina will recover with rest."

"How much rest?" I don't mean to sound like that, but there is a hard edge to my voice. Why would she risk so much for a woman she didn't even know? A woman who had no reason to call on her loyalty?

"She will need at least a couple of days, but I think she will be fine after that. The villagers told me there is one more village not far from here before we reach the summit. It is where people go to heal."

"Another place of the springs?"

"Yes, it is as good as the one in the valley, perhaps even better, though more remote."

Paul has come up behind me and protectively places a hand around my waist.

"I feared this to be true." Jacob's voice is hoarse and it sends a pang of fear through me.

"What?"

"Since I saw the thief in our camp, I knew Ute's powers were being encouraged, helped along by the Evil One as they were in the past. He can possess those who have not been guarded by the Holy One, who have not taken his Spirit in and been forgiven for their sins."

I feel my face bunch in wrinkles. "Are you saying that those not guarded and forgiven stand in danger of being used by the Evil One, possibly possessed by the sorceress?"

"It is the way of things. Think about what we learned from the thief and the possessed family. They were not followers of the Christ. They had vulnerable areas."

"How does one guard against that?" Paul pulls me tighter against him.

"We must remember that we do not fight against what we can see, the people we live with, the people we encounter. No, it is the spirit of the Evil One who contends against the Spirit of the God Most High."

"If we follow God, we are protected?"

"We will still come under attack, and I am afraid that the farther we go on this journey, the harder the Evil One will attack us. We must remember to shield ourselves with our faith in God, protect our minds with the salvation he has provided through the sacrifice of his Son. We must hold up our faith like a shield against the doubts fired down on us, stand firm in each step we take to share his salvation, putting on the truth like a belt and protecting our hearts with his righteousness. We must remember his words to us and use them like a sword."

"What if we don't know his words?" I didn't mean to say that aloud, and now that the words are out, everyone looks at me.

"You know some of it, Rapunzel. Do you believe it to be true?"

I look away from the expectant stares, looking only into my mother's green eyes as she lies prone, weak after the beating. "Sometimes I think I do, but there are other times I doubt he is good, that he is who he says he is. Sometimes I feel as though perhaps there is no difference between him and Ute. He has allowed so many things in this broken world."

"But he has promised to redeem it. That's why the Son of God came."

"But if he has come already, why isn't this pain finished now?"

"He is at work, and he is not finished with what he has

begun. We are in the middle of a story, Rapunzel. He will return to call his people home and make all things new."

"When?"

"When he does. We should be patient. His timing is not ours."

Oh, these platitudes! I stop talking. There is nothing I can say that everyone will understand. There are no words I can use to explain my frustration with this God that I sometimes feel called to and other times feel vexed by. How can I feel this way for the one who I think created me? Why can I not resolve this?

BARGAINING

After a few days of rest, we begin again. We must go at a slow pace for my mother, but we cannot leave her behind in that strange village. But after two days of travel, we must take another day to rest. My mother's face is rigid with pain when Jacob helps her down from her horse. His eyes are dark with worry and he shakes his head at Paul. "We can't keep going like this."

I know he is right, but I feel strange at seeing how he cares for her. He fusses over her as we ready ourselves to eat, making sure she is comfortable. Despite her pain, she smiles at him.

Supper is quiet. We have run out of stories to tell. All around us the night air is heavy with something I can't name. When we lie down to rest, I cannot sleep. I feel as though I can hear movement, but it doesn't seem to be a sound. The sound of owls catching rodents has ceased. There is something stealthy moving its large body this way. I glance up at Amis who is nodding by the fire, and I shake with fright when a growl disrupts the quiet.

Paul is already up beside me. "What is it?" I ask him.

"It's a mountain lion. Don't worry—I've told you they don't approach when the flames are high." He rises to send a sleepy Amis to his bedroll and puts more wood on the fire. "I will sit up, you will be safe."

"I'm sorry . . ." Amis mumbles as he goes.

"It's fine," Paul says with a sigh. "Go back to sleep, Rapunzel. I'll keep you safe."

I begin to nod off, but wake to a growl coming closer and closer.

Paul is lunging with his sword as the teeth of a mountain lion open wide and come snapping at him. "Paul, watch out! Be careful!" But the animal leaps into the air, ready to claw him. Paul stabs it through the belly, its entrails spilling out like a rope uncoiling. Though it yelps and falls to the ground, it doesn't stay down. The thing doesn't know it should be dead—it rises again. He slashes through its throat and blood spurts. The animal gurgles and sprays Paul with a fine mist of blood before finally falling prostrate at his feet.

Dashing forward, I grab my husband. Pulling him close, I take in a deep breath as tears wet my face. "You're alive!" I splutter.

"You didn't think I'd let it kill me, did you?" He pushes me back and laughs at the look on my face. "I wouldn't leave you in the mountains to face Ute alone."

He kisses me on the mouth and I don't care if the blood gets all over me, I just want him to be safe. I want to be away from curses and spells and witches and sorceresses. I know in my heart that she possessed the beast, she caused this to happen. I'm not surprised when Ute's image flickers in the air above us.

"Well, well, well, in the heat of the moment you can make a decision, can't you, little man? You can fight for your life, you can save others—but do you know what else to do? Do you see what is ahead?" Her voice fills the night before thunder claps and a downpour drenches our fire. As we rush to find shelter beneath nearby trees, I think that at least the rain will wash away the blood.

⊂⊛⊃

WHEN I LIE DOWN, the snarls and growls from the attack sound like a gong in my mind. I try to rest on the cold, needled floor, but I can't sleep. Ute's not through with her visit.

Defying the dark of the night, she floats high above me, glowing malevolently. "You wanted to stay safe from me, didn't you, little Rapunzel? You thought taking a little trip into the wood in that valley would help. But you see what happens to people when you to try to delay things and change your course even a little bit? First, those women were hurt, then your mother, and tonight, I almost took your husband from you. I can do this and so much more than you ever dreamed if you don't continue your journey. No further delays."

"I am coming—we stopped in the wood because we needed food."

"The food was an excuse. You'll have as much as you need as long as you come to me. Do you really think I would let you go hungry on the trail? There is plenty for you. You should have continued coming to me straightaway."

"We did! My mother first needed time to recover."

"Perhaps you should have left her behind and allowed me to see to her needs."

"You possess sisters to make them kill each other! Why should I trust you?"

"Because I have plans for you, I have things for you to

do, and I will provide what I must to make certain you are safe until you get to me."

My mouth is stuck and I can't say anything. How do I fight her? The pull she has on me leaves me aching all over.

"You want to tell Paul about these dreams, don't you? That would not be wise, little girl."

"Why?"

"He will try to stop you from coming. You must not tell him. You must not tell him, or more people will get hurt."

"Stop it! Leave them alone, I'll come to you."

"Promise me! Promise you won't divert and you won't tell Paul."

"I promise, but my mother is struggling—"

"Don't try to make bargains with me!" But something shifts in her expression. "I know you won't break your promise. Fine, I'll allow you a little time to help her heal— there's a place up ahead—but only a little while. Under- stand?" Her lips stretch in a wide, leering smile. "You see? I can be kind if you only ask. You should always ask before you do anything. I don't *want* to hurt your friends—I simply want you to join me. Just keep coming and we will get along."

I hear the shrill wind blowing and I shudder. What is she doing now, and why can't I stop her? Are my secrets hurting us? What will my compliance cost now?

THE WEB

ach morning that we wake, we are covered in a mist, a fog. The air is cold and wet with a heaviness—and I can't stop thinking about my witch. How she loved to use the mist to confuse those around us! As the moisture clings to my hair each morning, I feel hazy and befuddled.

Paul doesn't seem to mind. "It will fade." He smiles and cups my cheek before a gentle kiss. "As long as I can see you, we will find our way. Each morning I am still astounded that you chose me and that you are my wife now. Don't worry, my Rapunzel, we will find our way."

But I know this feeling too well, I have been wound inside this web before. Over and over the questions rasps in my mind: What was my witch trying to teach me, and how was she "training" me? Perhaps if I told Paul the truth I've learned about who I am—but I cannot. What if it *is* all my fault? Are my desires creating this mist? Am I drawing us into something deeper, something darker? I'm not sure which way to go in my thoughts anymore. I feel scared all the time, as though my spirit quakes within me.

"Trust that God has his hand on us," Paul counsels me, and I know that I should. I should trust, I should believe, but though I try, I can't seem to.

⁓

"THERE WAS ONCE a man who thought he believed." When our monk begins this way tonight after we eat, I realize he and Paul have been discussing me. I look up at Paul with the question in my eyes, but he just nods. I try not to feel like a recalcitrant child.

Jacob is holding onto a small piece of wood, carving it as he speaks. I wonder what designs he is making. "The man had a child, a precious son that he loved more than he loved anything else in the world. Now, the child was possessed of a spirit that would make him foam at the mouth. The spirit would cause him to throw himself into the water to drown or into the fire to burn. Can you imagine how the father felt? He loved his son, but he couldn't do anything but watch his child constantly. He would catch him when he would fall, drag him time and time again out of the water, away from the fire. Perhaps his father stopped letting the boy go outside near the water, maybe his family stopped cooking their food for fear of what the spirit would make the boy do.

"At last, the father heard that the followers of the Lord Jesu were nearby. He took the boy and pled with them to heal him. Did he go to them because he thought nothing could be done for his son? No, of course not, but even though he believed, even though they believed, when they called on God, that he could save the boy, still there was something there that kept them from trusting completely. Though they tried everything they knew how, the spirit would not leave the boy.

"Jesu returned from a trip up the mountain and was told what his followers had tried. He rebuked their lack of faith, and the father cried out, 'I believe, help my unbelief!' And Jesu took that broken faith and cast out the demon, healed the boy. Do you know, because I doubt at times, I often think of this story. Can God use me, use us?

"This enemy we face is crafty, but she is just a tool for the true enemy. The enemy is stronger than us, but he is nothing compared to Jesu. But I admit, I still struggle. I believe—help my unbelief." He continues to whittle. "We will pray that God will increase our faith, that the Spirit of the Most High will guard and guide us. Perhaps together we will cry out, and He will answer our prayers."

⸲⸲⸲

I can't sleep, so I move away from the others and find her on a rock looking down the mountain. "Mother?"

She turns to face me, her bruised face lit by moonlight. Even that stilted motion shows how much pain she is still in. I hope that the place of healing ahead can help her. Her smile quirks. "Daughter?"

"Why aren't you sleeping? Are you hurting too much?"

She shakes her head, and her voice is low as she speaks into the night. I can see her breath form puffs of air. "I can't stop thinking. I'm not sure what to do with my life."

"Well, first let's stop a sorceress."

She laughs at this. "I meant after that."

I'm grateful she thinks there will be an after. I walk over and sit down next to her. "You'll come live with Paul and me, like we said before all this began."

"Do you still want me to?"

I look up at her, shocked. "Of course I do."

"Why?"

"Because you're my mother. I love you. I need you."

"Rapunzel, I don't feel like I have anything of worth to offer you. Only pain from what I did in the past to hurt you."

I shake my head. "No—without you, I don't think I would have been able to make it through this trip. Perhaps I haven't confided in you as I ought to have, but . . . I'm still learning how to do that."

She chews on this thought for a moment. "And what will I do when we reach the end of this journey?" I notice her shiver.

"Mother, I don't even know what I'll do. What do queens and the mothers of queens do? Travel their kingdoms? Solve mysteries?"

She laughs again. "We both know so little of normal life . . . I wish—"

The silence dangles as I stare into the shadows down below us. Do I want to know her wish? "What?"

"I wish I could start over. Begin again. Not as the foolish girl I was, but now, as a grown woman."

Her longing touches me, and I want her to have a normal life, but is it possible for any of us? "Would you marry again?"

Her hands pick at her dress and she avoids my eyes. "I don't think I can love the type of man who can love me back."

I don't want to know more, so I don't press further. "You have helped so much on this trip. Would you want to become a midwife?"

Her saucy grin shapes her mouth again, and she looks me full in the face this time. "Now that I think about it, yes. I could do that."

Silence descends again but for the sounds of nocturnal

scampering. I reach out and take her cold hand in mine and we sit like that, allowing our bodies to grow stiff in the cold even as our interlocked hands grow warm from our shared heat.

THE PLACE OF HEALING

It has taken us a few more days to arrive, due to our slow pace, but we are at last at a place of healing high in the mountains, just at the treeline. The family that hosts us is fascinating, and they know Paul well. I remember the tale Jacob told us of the cobbler and his wife who entertained angels unaware. I wonder about the people we stay with from place to place. So many have been happy to have us, and the hospitality is extraordinary to me. I can't imagine the witch ever opening up her home, though she had so much that she could have shared. She wouldn't even provide a door in her wall. What will Paul and I be like? Will we have a home that is kind to strangers? Will we be like Dorothea or these kind people who share whatever they have?

"Come inside," says the huge woman who opens the door. She is not like any Northland woman I have seen. Her hair is dark and curly with streaks of grey all through it. She has a red, weathered face that suits her brash voice. It is surprising that she is still close to Jacob's height despite the hunched way she holds herself. The fire warms us as we enter the cave dwelling, and I relish the heat after the cold wind blowing against us for days.

The woman doesn't even ask what we have come for, just begins unwinding our scarves from around us. Paul has explained that this is the way of the Soontrisse people when they share their hospitality, so we hold still while she does it. One by one, we shed our layers, but not before we have grown warm enough that we are grateful to lose them. Next, we are led a little farther in where we are invited to sit on a long, hard bench. Once seated, our feet receive the same care by the small children in the family. First the hard-soled boots come off, followed by our thick socks.

I can't help the expression that crosses my face as I worry over our smelly feet. The large girl who is helping me looks up with a smile, as though she knows my thoughts. "It is not so bad!" she laughs, and then puts my feet into a basin of warmed water. Oh, the bliss after walking and riding so far! I want to put my entire body into the small bowl, but of course I wouldn't fit. I'm sure I'm being ridiculous. As I sigh, I look closer at the girl. She is probably a few years younger than myself, and I notice that she keeps giving Paul side glances.

"Come with me," she says, and she leads me into another tiny room off to the side where she helps me undress. I feel shy; it is odd to take off all my clothes with others nearby. She takes my clothes and opens a door. As we step into this next room, the heat envelops me and I instantly begin to sweat. My mother—I try not to look below her chin—sits down with me, and we watch as steam rises. The travel of the past months begins to melt away from our forms. I'm not certain how long we sit there like that, taking in deep breaths, but the girl comes back and has us enter another room where we lie down on two tables. This room is also warm, but not as hot as the previous room. The girl is joined by her sister, and they work some sort of oil into our skin. My girl rubs until I find myself moaning. I feel myself blush, but the girl, whose large hands are so strong it is shocking, begins to laugh. "You were so quiet at first—I was afraid you could feel nothing. It is good to make noises so that I know what helps and what hurts. This is a place of healing. We are here to help."

I feel the weariness of our journey come upon me and I begin to cry. My body shudders, wracked by sobs, but the girl doesn't leave me alone. She continues to rub and I finish my cry with a hiccup. I laugh. "Is that normal?"

"For some people. I would not worry about it, Your Highness."

"I am not a princess."

"But of course you are! You are married to Prince Paul. It is my privilege to serve you, and I am happy for anything I can do to make your way easier."

I feel silly for the pang of jealousy I felt earlier and now wish I could take her with me. Of course, I cannot. The way before me is cloudy, and I wouldn't want to take anyone with us except those I know can defend themselves. Perhaps that is why Paul seems so upset at times. Perhaps he doesn't think that I can defend myself . . .

I hiccup again and then laugh. The girl begins to scrape off the lotion—and a good bit of dirt, I imagine. She then has me return into the heated room. "Now you must go wash off in the springs. Your mother is already there. She left while you were composing yourself."

I feel the sadness pool inside me again as I think of

these kind people trying to aid others and a sorceress nearby causing harm. When I enter the springs, I look at my mother, her bruises apparent in the water. I wonder how much of a massage she could handle, but I don't remember her making any sounds. Something about her has softened, though, and for that I'm grateful.

After a long soak, the girls return to us and take us to yet another chamber. "They say that you have come to help us and free our king from the spell." My helper dries me off with the towel after rubbing a different lotion into my skin. After finishing, she wraps a fresh robe around me.

"Your clothes will be clean in the morning. Wear this till then. It is our gift to you."

Before we rise, our feet are dried and then put into loosely laced leather slippers lined with the softest lamb's wool. I feel a different person than the Rapunzel who has been traveling for weeks.

"You told me that the witch placed you in different places for her purpose." My voice is quiet and I can't help the tremble that quivers inside it as I lie next to my mother in the sleeping room reserved for women. "Did she send *me* where she wanted me to go?"

I hear her turn stiffly toward me, and I look at her in the dim light cast by a single candle. Her voice is husky as she says, "I can't say for certain everywhere she sent you, but yes, sometimes she did. Other times I think she just helped you along."

"Why would she want me to find Dorothea?"

"She didn't—she wanted you to find Nicholas."

I shiver. "Why would she want me to find Bluebeard?"

"That is obvious. He tried to kill you, didn't he?"

"But how could she have known that? Was she really so powerful?"

"Or perhaps she knew you that well."

I nod, contemplative. "Yes, she did, didn't she? Do you really think I disrupted Ute's plans?" I wonder how much my mother knows; are there things she knows that she won't say? With my head bowed slightly, I look up at her. What does she know that she's not saying?

"She had plans she never discussed with me."

"But what of the plans she did discuss with you?"

My mother stares at me, unblinking. "You think she told me things?"

"Of course she did. She taunted you, tortured you, you said."

"I was a cat for twenty years. That was torture. I lost my husband, that was torture. She had my child and I never knew what all she did to you—that was unending torture."

"But what did she say she would *do* with me?"

My mother shifts away.

"Come now, mother, I know that she had plans for me —everyone does. What were her plans?" I need to hear her say it. I need to know.

She turns back to me and reaches for me with un-catlike trembling hands. "She said she would make you just like her. She said she could twist you and turn you and use your powers to—"

"My what?"

"Your powers."

"I don't have powers."

"You are wrong, Rapunzel, you do." She snaps her mouth shut. Time seems to suspend itself, and I'm not sure I can breathe. I take a breath, and another, over and over again, but I cannot breathe deeply. Around my field of vision in the darkness, little lights start to blink. I continue to struggle, continue to forget how to breathe properly.

"Rapunzel?" She places her hands on either side of my

head. "Rapunzel, listen to me. Breathe in slowly through your nose and back out through your mouth." I try to, but I can't slow down. "Take in a slow, slow breath through your nose and slowly let it go through your mouth."

My head feels as though it will burst. I stare at her in the darkness, I can't quite understand what she is saying, but I concentrate on the sound of her voice. "Listen to me, listen to me—she wanted to control you, but she couldn't. No one can. You make your own choices. God has made you who you are, no matter how she wanted to manipulate and pollute you. You must decide what to do."

I reach out and grab her. "Don't tell Paul—" I choke out. It takes a moment, but I am slowly getting my breath back. "Don't tell Paul!" He mustn't know, mustn't guess. If he does, he will never look at me the same again.

"Rapunzel, you need to tell him. Talk to him, he's a good man."

It is awhile before I can respond. My head hurts so much I think I will cry, but instead I look at her. Something in me lashes out. "I know Paul is a good man, that's why I married him. So was my father, but did you talk to him? Did he understand who your sister was and what you really wanted?"

She hangs her head. "I didn't even know what I really wanted."

"So you didn't talk to him?"

"He knew bits and pieces—but he kept things from me, too."

"Then don't tell me how to handle my husband."

"Rapunzel—"

But I turn my back on her. I shove my hand over my mouth, how could I—I can feel her weeping behind me, her shoulders shaking in silent regret, but I don't turn over. I just let the hot tears flow until I fall asleep.

cᗊஇᗌ

THE NEXT DAY we are back to climbing higher and higher, searching for signs of this enchanted castle Paul grew up hearing stories about. The day is long and the ride is tiring, and evening finds us sitting mute in front of the flames after eating. I look around at my companions. I am wrong to be sitting here; my very wrongness must be apparent to all around me. It is the reason that I cannot speak with my mother or Paul without causing problems. Even if I decide not to say anything, it still comes out causing harm. They say there is a purpose, but I can't understand what that would be.

cᗊஇᗌ

PAUL IS STARING VERY hard into the flames tonight. I imagine he is thinking he should never have married me. Why did I think I could live a normal life, that it would make me happy? I wasn't raised for it. Apparently I was raised to one day become a witch, one day perhaps even raise my status to that of a sorceress of the grandest order —like Ute herself. Would it be easier to be evil than to fight it? I think of the child, Jesu, who came into this world to save us from ourselves, to reunite us to God, Jacob says. Where did it all go wrong?

Was the witch right all along? But no, I know how bitter she was, how hateful. I know how she despised the world of men, and I can't ever want to be like that, no matter how alluring power might seem. Sometimes I do think if I just had a bit of power, I could fight a bit better, I could free this land from its curse, I could—but I hear myself and I grow a bit sick. "I, I, I"—over and over it is *I* that I am thinking of, it is *I* that I think can fix all things.

Haven't I yet seen that I cannot do these things, that I am helpless in the face of all of this? But here I am, traveling down the same worn path, thinking the same worn thoughts. I look away from the flames, but the light has made an impression on my vision.

LIVING WATER

The sunrise is astounding in all its glory. The sky is
filled with a vibrant pink that is shot through
with bright orange and yellow. The sparse clouds are
outlined in gold and rays of light seem to burst out as the
sun rises behind them. I breathe in the cool air as I stare
over the edge of the trail, careful not to look down the
steep mountainside.

Paul startles me and I jerk out of my reverie. "Be careful," Paul cautions, catching me around the waist. "I don't
want you to fall. I don't want to lose you."

"How could you lose me?" I try to smile, but my mouth
is stiff. Physically he is holding me, but the weight of uncertainty wedges between us. How can we talk, how can we
say anything? I can never let him know that his father is
right—there is something about me that could destroy the
kingdom.

Does Jacob sense this? Does he know that my coming
along is because I was being trained to be the next apprentice? I was raised to be twisted into something—I don't
even comprehend what kind of training Ute implied I was

receiving. The stories that I feasted on while living in my tower run through my mind. They did have a strong thread of power and, of course, sorcery was highly thought of in them. Witches were not evil in those books . . . Are they inherently evil, or is it the greed that makes them so? My mind lingers on this question.

I think of the idolatry we each seem to harbor. I long to be normal and prove my worth, Paul wants to prove his, my mother wants to reconcile herself and make up for her past, Jacob wants to save us all, and Amis—what is it that our own little Amis wants? He wants to serve. Perhaps he is the purest of us all.

I hear Paul's caution. "We must break fast if we are to find her today. We must not allow any weakness to show. She will test us and try to break us apart."

Oh, Paul, are we already broken?

c∂∞∞∞

THE RIDE to the summit will be chilly, and my hands are stiff even wearing my gloves while eating. Jacob says that in some mountains climbing ropes are necessary, but the place we are going to does not have an actual peak on it, only a rise where sacred runes and a sacrificial altar rest.

"An altar?" I ask between my bites of tough bread.

"Did you never see one?"

I think of all the things the witch allowed me to witness: growing her herbs, mixing her smelling potions, memorizing her many spells, practicing her stories. "No, there were no altars." I state firmly, scared a bit that my mind may not remember something important. What if she had hidden it from me—but is she so powerful that she could come into my mind and change my memories? Even now that she is dead, does she still have a hold over me?

I glance at Jacob. He is staring at me, but he breaks his usual character to give me a half-smile. "I suppose you would remember something like that."

"Would I?"

He nods, as though to encourage me. "I think you would."

"She would want you to doubt yourself, daughter," my mother cautions, and rests a hand on my shoulder.

I struggle not to jerk away. "How can I not?" Especially now that I know that she was training me for something more than what I fathomed. My mother locks me in her gaze and refuses to look away from my shame.

I will make this right, I must. I feel the anger quickening inside me once more, the injustice of being manipulated and lied to all of my life. Never having had a proper upbringing with a loving father and mother, proper rearing in the church . . . What kind of woman would I be now, had I had those things?

We continue our trek up the mountain but make a stop when we come to a small clearing near evening. The climb is taking longer than Jacob and Paul had thought. The group settles down before it grows too dark and we chew on the tough leather of venison we brought from the healing springs. I am glad it is not dried fish. I am sick to death of it, though I should not complain because it gave us sustenance. I finish off the meal with a bit of dried fruit and swish down some water. But I refill and empty my water bladder at the river twice, never feeling satisfied. As we have ascended, the river seems to have shrunk. If only my thirst would, as well.

"Christ called himself *living water* when he was here on the earth," Jacob muses.

My mother turns her green eyes on him. "I'd forgotten that."

Jacob gives her the slow smile only she can pull from him. "There was a woman who went out at the hottest part of the day to fetch her water."

"That sounds a foolish thing to do." Her saucy grin seems to amuse our stern monk.

"Well, it sounds foolish to us, but she probably did it to avoid the other women."

"Why would she be avoiding them?" I question.

"She had made horrible choices with her life. She had been married to five different men and was living with another at that time. I doubt the other women liked her or had anything nice to say to her."

"Oh!"

"Yes, 'Oh!' If you feel that kind of judgement for her, just imagine what others thought of her, the ones who knew her."

I can imagine.

"Christ asked her for a drink, which surprised her. Men like him didn't speak to people like her, especially not women. When they began to converse, she thought perhaps he was a prophet, but he revealed he was much more than that. He illustrated that he was the living water, and whoever came to him would never be thirsty again."

I ponder what it would be like if we were on this journey and never needed to drink, never needed to water the horses, never needed to take the time to clean ourselves. What if all our needs had indeed been met by this Son of God? What if he was indeed the water that would slake our thirst and rid us forever of the need? We would not have to go and fight this sorceress. If he were who he said he was, he could take care of her before we even got halfway to the cliffs. Why didn't he?

"He was able to tell the woman who she was and the

things she had done to waste her life. He gave her hope—and from that point on, she never thirsted again."

"She never had to go for water again?"

"I'm not speaking of a physical thirst."

"Of course not." I can't stop the sarcastic tone from taking over my voice. "Does he ever meet our physical needs?"

I don't like the hurt look I see cross Paul's face. "Rapunzel, wait. He provided me with you. He has given us Jacob who has helped us with which way to go. He reunited you with your mother—"

Whom I keep hurting, I think.

"And what of me? I am your biggest blessing, for without me, you would never laugh!" Amis jokes, but for once he cannot lift my spirits.

I shake my head, "I'm sorry—I must just be tired. It's hard to know what to think about this God when we are here fighting a sorceress so powerful." Perhaps if I could explain how she visits me—I know my mother thinks I should. I can see it in her expression. She understands mistakes; she doesn't want me to make this one. I start to open my mouth.

"I was hoping we would have found her by now." Paul's confession has a sense of regret about it. My mind won't rest. It seems to pull at his words as though to find a secret beneath them.

I feel there is something here he has been keeping from us. There is something he hasn't discussed with me, one of the things that I've seen him talking about with Jacob and even Amis. I look at my mother—does she feel left out, too? I notice she is batting away a snowflake descending. I nearly laugh in distraction, but anger and frustration pull at me again.

All of me hurts, and I'm just so tired and so very, very

thirsty. If only Christ would give me this living water so I could never thirst again.

Why won't my own husband talk to me? First it was all that nonsense with his father, and now it seems I am locked out of all his decisions. If my mother and I are supposed to be such a vital part of this plan, shouldn't we help strategize? A thought brings me to a halt. Does he know somehow he shouldn't trust me, like his father said?

I try to calm down. I know that he can't discuss everything with me and that I know almost nothing of going up into a mountain, but still . . . I feel almost like a little girl, and there is a peevishness about my attitude that makes me ashamed. I am grateful no one can hear my thoughts, no one can know what I'm really wanting to do, which is run off by myself right now.

FRAGILE

I back away and wander down the trail a ways, even though it really is getting too dark to do so. No one says anything to me, not even my mother who is batting at the snow. Fluffy stuff keeps clinging to my lashes and making it hard to see as it floats down.

Ute's appearance should not surprise me. How does she know when I'm most vulnerable?

"Where are your friends?"

"Discussing things."

"Things that don't concern you?"

"Of course they concern me."

"Then why aren't you part of the discussion?"

I stare at her apparition—her long flowing dark-purple cloak is of deep velvet, but its edges seem to fade away as though her image is a bit smeared in the gloaming. I wipe at my eyes, thinking the snow has clouded my vision, but it's not that at all, it's her.

Her white hair reaches down to her waist. The tresses are thick, falling over her shoulders in straight, shining locks. Her obsidian eyes stare at me. "What do you think,

Rapunzel, are you coming closer like I want you to? Are you sure that you wish to continue on this track?"

"You told me I should—that if I do, I will give you what you want."

She laughs, a hollow, rattling thing. "That you will, but I am surprised you have not discussed things with your beloved Paul."

"But you told me not to."

She stares at me and does not blink for a full minute. She simply shimmers in the air.

I take a deep breath. I know what she is saying to me. "And Paul does discuss things with me."

"I never said he didn't. Of course he includes you in anything that he feels you have a part to play in. But it is only natural, now that he is your husband, that he should make the choices for you. It is only natural that you should follow him. It's the right thing, isn't it?" Again she stares at me without blinking. She could play this staring game with my mother, and who knows who would win?

"I trust Paul."

"Why wouldn't you?"

"He trusts Jacob."

"Of course he does."

"They are only doing what they feel is best."

"I would expect nothing less."

I squirm beneath her gaze.

"Just one question. If you trust him so much, dear one, then why not tell him of our little conversations?"

"I just said—you told me not to say anything."

"And you obeyed like a good little girl."

Before I can retort, she has vanished. All her smears of color are gone.

⚭

When I return to the group, Paul pulls me away from the others to go sit by ourselves. Perhaps I was missed. As the stars dot the sky, he begins to speak and turns me toward him. "We will reach the summit tomorrow. We have to." He looks at me and traces a finger down my face. "I'm sorry."

"What? I mean, why?"

"This—this, everything has been so hard. Not what I wanted for us. I'm sorry, Rapunzel, but I know it will get better. I love you."

I stare up at him, wishing we were near the fire so I could see his face more clearly, but grateful for the privacy all the same. "I love you, too."

A sigh escapes him.

"What is it?"

"Perhaps if you had married a different man, you would be safe inside your own home."

"Perhaps, but it would not be you and I am sure it would not be me."

"What do you mean?"

"I don't think I could ever marry anyone but you, my love. Who else could know me as you do?" He frowns and looks away, so I touch his arm. "What?"

"But I don't feel I know you at all. Every time I think I know you, there is something more about you that is revealed. There is so little about your time with the witch that you have shared—"

I stiffen at this, but he continues as though he doesn't notice.

"—and I don't know what all you are keeping secret."

"You think I keep secrets from you?"

"Perhaps not on purpose, my love, but you don't share whole pieces of yourself. We are supposed to be one,

Rapunzel, we are supposed to share things and know each other."

"Just as you have shared about your father, about your mother? I am not the only one to keep secrets." This tongue of mine! It was better when I didn't speak at all.

"I do not keep anything from you that would hurt you—"

"It does hurt me, Paul. It hurts me that you won't tell me what your father has done and said to make you—" But I don't know what to say.

"To make me what?"

"Why can't you speak of him?"

"To make me less?"

"What do you mean, less?"

"I know what my father thinks of me, what he has always thought of me until he needed me. But what do you think of me?"

"I love you!" I spit out with heat. There is no sound of love in my tone.

"Do you really? You would be here with me no matter what? Even if I was not to inherit a kingdom?"

"No."

His eyes widen.

"We would neither of us be here if you weren't sent by your uncle to protect the kingdom you are inheriting."

"You know what I mean."

"I would be with you no matter what. I have loved you since before I knew you to be a prince. I have told you I'm not even sure that I want to be a queen."

He looks down at his strong hands. "I thought I could hold you, that together we could be what God desired of us, but you are elusive. You will not meld with me, Rapunzel, you hold yourself away from me."

I don't know what to say. Perhaps there is nothing to

say. Though we share the same blanket at night, I wonder if it is only because of the cold. My feet walk away from his warmth. I am colder and miss his touch, but I cannot will myself to turn back to him. My back turns to him and I stand, lonely, aching, the hot tears quickly chilling little rivers on my face. I hiccup. Oh, how I hate the sound!

Paul comes to me and puts his arms around me, and I cry harder. He leans in and kisses my hair. "Even if you hold yourself apart, I will still love you, my wife. You are mine and I am yours. You are part of me and always will be."

"I'm your rib?" I try to laugh, but it falls flat.

"Jest if you must, but you are that much a part of me."

"Then why . . ." But I can't speak. My throat is closing up against all the words that long to come out. I can't think; the exhaustion is too much, and I feel pulled into the darkness, even though she may be waiting there for me again.

THE SUMMIT

This final trail is the steepest, but at least we don't have to scale a cliff. If Ute were on the peak opposite us to the north of King Onfroi's valley, we would have to. I hope against hope that we haven't misunderstood and hiked up the wrong one. Each step is a lunge, and as I pull myself up higher and higher, the air sears my lungs with its sharp cold. It feels thin and I get a bit dizzy. I think my mother struggles as well, since I have seen her shake her head as though trying to stabilize herself.

"We need some food and rest," Paul says to me as we slow down for a short break.

I moan as I lower myself to the ground.

"Imagine if you were on this journey at my age," my mother says with a laugh.

"You are not so very old." I smile. "I believe that being a cat kept you young."

"That and eating mice," Amis quips.

Paul laughs at this. "I never knew that eating mice could help women stay young."

"Now you know! You'd best catch some for Rapunzel to keep her young."

My mother looks ahead. We are following a trail that has diminished the higher we have travelled. It has all but disappeared. "Who would come this way?"

Jacob stands nearby. "Only those that were going to the sacred stones. There is a much faster trail skirting the summit that leads to Alleria."

"Is the altar where you think the castle is?"

"It is where I know she is," Jacob states.

My mother looks like she would argue this with anyone, but not Jacob. "How do you know it is here?"

"I came when it was smashed. My brothers and I were very young and it was some time after the War of Sorcery, but I remember one morning being woken up by a horrible dream. I couldn't remember any of it. I grabbed my father confessor and told him what I could remember at first. The entire brotherhood began to pray.

"We knew at that time there had been many sacred places where they practiced their craft. Right after the war, most were destroyed, but this one was out of the way—and though it was a place of great power, very few knew of its existence. I had to describe the dream in detail to the elder monks. There was a monk who had grown up in the Northlands, in Trisse, actually. After days of fasting, he was able to piece together where in the mountains it was. Then the monks choose a few to go, and I was one.

"We travelled the southern route through the waters and made our way to Trisse without pirates stopping us. As we went higher and higher, I remember how I coughed, trying to take deep breaths, not realizing how thin the air would get. I had lived all my life by the bayous in the Eastern Ports, where that hot, salty depth was such a contrast to this icy chill. And the people we came across were so different from us—not just the language or their complexion, but so loud and expressive. Only in our music do we feel that freedom in the Eastern Ports. Music frees our souls to worship, to dance, to triumph!"

He shakes his head as though processing the sounds from the past. "At last we arrived, and we ascended, singing psalms of triumph over our enemy. She appeared to us, roaring. I'll never forget how she looked—ice-white hair and skin, charcoal-black eyes. She wanted us gone, but she had no power, and we cast her out and cracked the great altar. There should be no power left there now."

He frowns a moment before continuing, his dark eyes focused on Paul as though no one else can hear. "That trip changed the trajectory of my life. I never returned to my homeland but spent the rest of my time training to become a warrior monk in Trisse. I grew up with your uncle and knew your mother before she married and was taken away. I thought I was tainted by my mother's sins of trusting in witchcraft and sorcery. That I had to pay for her wrongs with my life. I pushed so many people away when I chose this life.

"I was wrong. The God I know now offers peace and freedom, even in the midst of difficulties and trials. I know what we are to do now seems impossible, but we will see it through. We will stop her at the source of her power."

Amis tilts his head and clears his throat. "But you said, 'There should be no power there now.'" His imitation of Jacob's stern voice causes us all to laugh.

"She has found a new source of power and so must have revived the place." He looks at all of us in turn. "Let's finish this."

UTE SHOULD BE HERE, on the summit where the sacred stone rests with its runes carved deep into its cold slab. But the place is deserted, and the wind whips around our heads, making me wait for the sound of my witch's laugh. Will I ever forget how she would use the wind to taunt me, her voice rattling me as she spouted questions? She made me tremble with fear. I could not decide how to live my life for so long—but here I am, trying to live it with the man I love and want to trust. Trying to save a people I am just now learning about, with a mother I want to love and forgive. We must try.

But the slab lies before us, cracked down the middle, its pieces overturned and rough edges smoothed by the wind. There is no evidence of it having been used in the recent past. There is nothing here to suggest there has been a fire or anyone living nearby. All at once, her voice rises on the wind. "You thought it would be so simple, didn't you, little fools? You have come such a long way, and yet you still have such a long way to go."

Paul is looking all around, and Jacob has raised his staff into the air. Both men are circling our little group, driving my mother and me into the center. I am grateful we left Amis with the horses down the rise. "What is it you want?" Paul's voice is clear, deep, but she is laughing at him as she did in my dreams.

"Exactly what you are giving me. Right, little Rapunzel? Keep coming, and you will find me—and I promise that what you have will be enough."

"Enough for what?" Jacob booms.

"Oh, warrior monk! You think you can cast your prayers like a spell to conquer me? You think your god will vanquish me forever if you say just the right thing or do the right thing? Your god is nothing and he cannot contain the magic of this world. He cannot—"

"Be silent in the name of Jesu!" His shout echoes among the peaks, and I look at him in frustration.

When it is clear that she is gone, I can no longer contain my anger. It boils up like heated metal and spills over the cauldron of my mouth. "Why did you do that?" Jacob and Paul look at me with mouths slack. "We needed to know where she wanted us to go next—why did you stop her from speaking?"

Jacob shakes his head. "We will figure out where to go ourselves, Rapunzel."

"We are at an abandoned outpost for a sorceress who knows how to lure us forward. We are dancing on the edge of her spell, stumbling into her trap—"

Paul reaches for me. "Which is why Jacob stopped her from casting more of her spell on us."

I step backward. "We need to hear her to know *what* to avoid. To know what it is she wants of us so that we can discern where *not* to go, how *not* to proceed."

"Rapunzel, I know you are upset, but we will find our way."

I want to believe Paul, I want to trust that the instructions he and Jacob have given were right—but something within me tells me what we are doing is wrong, that every step on this path is leading to destruction.

"I must be alone to pray," Jacob states firmly. "I know God will show me the way."

The beauty of the day has failed me. The sun is lowering in the sky, and all I can see are the clouds gathering.

As we start down the trail, my mother reaches for my sleeve. "You should tell them," she says in a near-whisper. I look at her and give her a half-nod. Perhaps she is right.

We give Jacob time and join Amis a little way down from the summit. The horses are jittery; I can only assume the clouds overhead account for it. We make a fire for the evening and wait. As soon as Jacob returns, I will tell them —but as I look around at the faces of this strange little traveling group, it's funny, everyone looks a little odd, as though their coloring is changed. They seem to be almost green. I feel light-headed, and my head aches. My mother glances at me and then turns her full attention to me. "Rapunzel!" Her yelp is the last thing I hear before hitting the ground.

WITHIN

I hear the wind again. It is groaning around us. There is a darkness pressing in on me, and then a light comes near. I see the pink through the back of my eyelids. "Rapunzel?" A voice is calling my name, but I feel so heavy, so weary. If I open my eyes, will I be able to go on? Will we be able to find whatever it is we are looking for? What *are* we looking for?

Suddenly I remember: we are looking for what has poisoned the kings of the Northlands. What is sowing its deep root into the land in order to set Ute free? What is at work here that could reunite her to her sisters?

I hear dripping. Plip, plip, plip, plop. Plip, plip, plop. My mother's voice begins humming along with the little drips. I feel like I am wavering in a strange marriage of sounds and sights. I see before me the witch as she was, frazzled and bent with the weight of power. She is bowing to Ute, who is hovering above her, and they both begin to laugh.

I wake with a start. My mother is holding my hand in

her cold one, but she releases me as I sit up. The dripping continues, and I sense an echo at work. "Where are we?"

"As you fainted, Paul found us shelter inside this cave. We are lucky to have found our way inside before a storm hit."

"Snow?" I nearly moan. If I knew how to pray, I would ask for God to deliver us from this height safely. Surely he would not want us to die up here.

"Rapunzel, we will be fine. Jacob found us before it grew bad. The men know what to do during a snowstorm."

"Really? And do they know how to defeat a sorceress within her lair?" Even as I say it, I regret the harsh, bitter tone that comes out of my mouth. Is this who I am now?

"Rapunzel, we—we will find our way. I know it." She repeats Paul's phrase and I know she is right. We haven't come this far for nothing, but I find myself crying. My mother reaches out and I let her put her arms around me. I sob into her neck, ashamed of the tears that are pouring out of me, ashamed of the anger that I have poured out on her. I hate to cry, to feel so helpless, so lost. She rubs my back gently, and I take in her smell. Like me, she is in need of a bath, but something about her scent comforts me. I hiccup and laugh at my odd noises. She laughs as well, and I realize she has been crying, too.

"Why are you crying?" I sniffle at her.

"I feel helpless. I feel lost."

We feel the same?

"I don't even know why I've come, Rapunzel. What good have I been to you while we have been on this journey?"

Pictures of her throughout our trip come to me: her aid in helping me after my fall, her tender care when we came across the burn victims, her compassion as she covered the possessed woman with her body and tried to save her. Her words come to me, and at last I realize . . . she has been a *mother* to me. Her words and actions have encouraged me to keep nothing hidden from my husband, to persevere, to know we are better together. But I don't know how to say this, and even as I start to put the puzzle pieces together, discouragement descends. We have not completed our mission and I have not told my companions of our true danger. My head aches, so I rub my temples slowly. "I don't really know what we're doing, Mother. I know we need to find our way to stop this sorceress, but how can we—"

"I think we will find her here." Jacob interrupts as he approaches through the gloom. I look up to see that all three men are standing in front of us. Paul's eyes look at me, pained. He looks away quickly. "I think we need to explore the cave together if you are well enough."

"Why?"

"I believe the source of her power can be found here."

I shake my head. "I thought we were looking for her castle—" Of course, the men have already discussed this, since they have decided our course of action.

I shake my head again. Is this what she wants? I look around at the darkness gathering, now that a storm rages outside. Of course this is what she wants. There will be no room for retreat if we proceed.

"I don't like the idea of going inside any further," I state flatly.

"I've never explored a cavern like this before." Amis laughs to loosen the tension. "I will be glad to see what we discover as the magic reveals itself."

There is no use arguing; we are proceeding as the men have planned. Why did they even bring us along?

We leave the horses hobbled near a pool of water, and

each of us takes a pack to follow Paul into the caverns. I watch in fascination as the flame from the torch he carries causes shadows to jump and leap across the jagged edges of the cavern walls.

Where would a sorceress hide herself? We make our way in and through dark tunnels. The walls are cold and damp, which explains the dripping sound. The caverns seem to stretch on forever, a network of nooks and alcoves and winding trails. It feels like hours as we roam, but as we go, things change. The walls become smooth stones, and I recognize the ground beneath becoming level, as though we are in a fine dwelling of some sort. These are no longer cavern tunnels we are following but winding hallways traveling deeper and deeper into the heart of an enchanted mountain castle.

Paul finally says we must rest for the night.

"Shouldn't we light a fire?" my mother asks. We have only two torches the men have carried in. I can tell my mother is shivering, and I understand. The deeper we go, the more chilled I find myself.

Amis laughs in his good-natured way. "I would be only too happy to kindle a fire for you, my lady, but where shall I get the tinder from? I did not trek wood in here." He is right. Despite my frustration with Paul, I huddle near him for warmth. I am grateful for his large body, his mass and heat. His body gives me comfort, and I think again we must get past our misunderstandings. We will find a way to continue to love each other, to become stronger. I try not to listen to the voices that rumble beneath it all, that there is something wrong with the foundation of our marriage—or maybe something wrong with me.

We chew our dried provisions and drink our water in silence until Amis begins to chuckle.

Paul smiles, though it looks more like a sneer the way

the torch lights up his face. "Should I ask what it is that amuses you?"

"Of course you should ask, but are you prepared for the answer?" He chuckles again, and the sound reverberates around us.

"I don't think any of us are ever ready for the answers you give us." Jacob's sharp voice betrays how fatigued he is.

Amis laughs again, undisturbed by Jacob's sarcasm. "Tonight has me thinking of a young girl I met once. She was a strange thing, smiled when she was sad, cried when she was happy. I asked her why she was the way she was and she told me it was her mother's fault."

"Of course it was," I hear my mother mumble.

"When the girl was very young, before the War of Sorcery, long before the Church had become so vocal about their hatred of sorcery, the girl had to find her name."

"Why didn't she already have one?" I wonder aloud.

"She did, but it was lost. When she was born, the midwife was a witch. She had been a kind woman, and was trusted by those that lived in the village, but the Evil One seduced her to his side. Crafty thing, she began to steal the names of the babes that were born under her care. The parents were happy to have healthy children, but when they tried to name the little ones, the clunky names wouldn't fit. As the parents tried to call out the names, Geoffroi would become Georgius, and I suppose Rapunzel would become Regina. The children were aimless, lost themselves. As they would try to obey their parents, to feed the chickens or fetch water, they would trip over their feet, forget what they were about to do, and get lost in their own little yards. Heaven help them if they ventured out on their own, since they weren't able to find their way back."

I think of these children and their families. What would it be like to not ever allow your children out of your sight, to have them never grow up to help or be independent? What would it be like to be nameless and confused?

Amis has settled into the story now, leaning forward with a grin. Funny how his face always holds a glint of mischief. "When the girl was about your age, Rapunzel, she had never gone from home, never been away from her family. Her parents had other children—normal ones, as the witch had been found out and burned by this point."

I grimace.

"But one day the plague came. The whole family became ill, all except the girl. The only thing that could heal the family was an herb that grew out in the lands far, far to the south in the Eastern Ports. The girl was determined to help her family, so she took the family's plow horse and set off for the Eastern Ports. She had no sense of direction, but somehow God kept her moving ever southward. On the way she found companions, some good and some bad, and she had many adventures with them as she tried to discover what it was that she was to learn on the way. When she found herself in the Eastern Ports, she made her way to the marshy woodlands. There were no castles nearby, nor any villages. Everything that was built there kept sinking, so people stayed away.

"The girl was afraid of going there herself. She was used to the cold mountains in the Northlands, not the hot humidity that covered her with sweat till she was sticking to her clothes. She waded out into the marsh, her shoes now worn through, her hem several inches deep in the mire. Buzzing was loud in her ears as insects stung her, disrupting her focus. Why she had come, what she was trying to do? Only moments before, she had known something—but what was it? She couldn't remember anymore.

And then she heard someone calling to her. For the first time, she knew that voice.

"'What are you saying?' she cried out, but she heard nothing. She waited a few more heartbeats and called again, 'Is someone there? Do you know what it is that I am supposed to do?' Still there was no reply. Finally, with the last bit of energy she had, she called again, 'I don't know who you are, but do you know who I am?' A voice began singing, a clear, pure voice singing the girl's true name."

"What was her name?" I have to know.

"Rachel!" He laughs. "A little lamb, pure, she was able to return to her family because she finally knew who she was and what she was doing. She finally knew where she was going. When she returned home, she found that the plague had left her family blank. They couldn't smile when they were happy or cry when they were sad, so she cried for them and called them each by their names. When they heard her calling them, they listened to her and drank the drink she made for them with the algae from the marsh."

"It is an interesting story," Brother Jacob says, "but what is it supposed to teach us?"

"I don't tell stories to teach anything," says Amis as he lays out his bedding. I swear his eyes are twinkling. How did he know how to draw us in? This strange man, always helping us think of other things besides witches and grand sorcerers and warlocks, of fathers and mothers who cause problems because they are not perfect?

THE CASTLE CAVERN

There is much here that I don't understand, I think, as I continue to hear the sound of water plipping down. I can't get warm, and my mind is soaked in thoughts of defeat. I hear a strange mewling sound, reminding me so much of a cat that I turn to look over at my mother, but it's not her. It's good that we have left one torch burning in case any of us needs to rise in the middle of the night. I suppose we will always need to leave something burning as long as we are down here. We have to, or else we will be covered in a darkness so black we could not see our hands even if they were directly in front of our faces.

"You don't have to go on." Ute is floating above where I am sleeping next to Paul, and I can't help the scream that comes out of me. Paul wakes, and all of the others startle, "Oh, good, I was hoping you would all give me your attention." Her velvet, thick voice hums against the stone walls as she drifts through the air, hovering, showing us that she has mastered the art of mesmerizing us.

"You have it." Jacob is already on his feet with his staff

in hand. I see Paul steathfully moving to the side, holding his sword.

"Come now, brother monk, you do know that your staff won't cause me any harm, don't you? And you, Paul—you are no threat with your sword. No, none of you can hurt me."

I hear that strange sound again and realize by the look of puzzlement on the faces of everyone with me that they can hear it as well.

She smiles as though she has read my thoughts. "You poor child."

"I am not a child."

"Oh, but Rapunzel, you are; you can't make decisions—others have to make them for you. It is too bad that even though you allow them to do this," she says, scowling at Paul, "you don't actually trust them."

I ignore this last insult. "That might have been true at one time, but I decide for myself what to do. I know who to trust and why I should trust them. That is why I am here."

"I know, and the decisions that you make are excellent. They have led you to me, which is exactly where Eufemia wanted you to be."

"What do you mean?" Paul asks.

"Our Rapunzel hasn't told you, but now it's time you knew. Eufemia was training her to become mine. Rapunzel is the key to bringing my sisters back to myself, freeing us from this wretched curse that has so long imprisoned us. By bringing Rapunzel to me, Paul, you are helping your kingdom embrace the right king—who is actually a queen! It will be Rapunzel, but not the Rapunzel you thought you knew."

The mewling sound grows and echoes off the chamber's walls. Is it one cat or a dozen?

"Do you hear them?"

"Who?"

"My children. We searched for little ones for a long time, and Eufemia brought them to me, one at a time, until my power was ripe. Poor little things." She gestures as the torchlight grows brighter, revealing tiny skeletons littering the floor. "Some of them were even sacrificed directly to me to relieve an otherwise barren family. You met one family not that long ago, Rapunzel. Don't you remember Helga and her family, suffering with no children of their own? What a curse to endure for having offended a witch!" She gives a throaty laugh. "The only way to find your way free from offense is to give away your child. Isn't that right, Katterina?"

My mother's voice is strained. "Nothing will take away a witch's offense."

"Perhaps you are right. And Paul—your nephew has been a great help, and has outlasted so many!" She pulls out a skinny toddler and then a scrawny baby out of her long robe. The baby must have been born in the summertime. "They have each looked so fragile, so weak, but their strength has begun to set me free. What bliss!" She closes her eyes, tasting the sweetness of a dream coming to fruition. "Yes, and now their strength combined with that of Rapunzel's will at last give me what I crave."

Enough of this! "And how will you be able to sap my strength?"

Her eyes, black as night, shoot open. "Oh, no, you misunderstand, dear one! I will not sap your strength. I will not drain you as I have my little ones." Her voice is vile to my ears. "No, indeed. Your strength will replenish itself in the well deep within, and from it we will call my sisters back from afar. They will travel from the Eastern Ports and from the Illyan Sea, up the Ventrias, and find us here. Here, within the mountains, to the heart of my strength, where you will give them back their freedom!"

It doesn't matter that I don't understand how I can give them back their power; what matters is that even if I could, I never would. "Why do you think I would do that?"

She continues to cradle the babes to her chest while a knife appears in the air, pointing towards the babes. "Because you have been the sacrificed child, the child laid on the altar of another's greed. Each child was sacrificed for a purpose. Paul's nephew was given by King Onfroi to gain his power to subdue the other Northland kings. Of course, I stole the king's strength for my spell. And remember Helga, whose family bargained to free themselves from the witch's curse? This sweet little girl was hers, but I always collect my debts. Her family is no longer barren, but the cost was high. The lifeblood of these babes, like every babe I have taken, has given me the strength I needed to curse the kings. If you will not do as I ask, then I will end these little lives to do it."

"You would kill this small babe?" She is so tiny, frail, not the fat thing she should be at her age.

I look into Ute's black eyes. She nods at me, the jagged knife glittering next to the whimpering babes. "I will kill them both."

Jacob begins to raise his staff and cry out—but I won't let him. "No!"

He looks at me in disbelief.

"I will go with her."

"Rapunzel!" I can see that Paul and Jacob have some plan, some way they think they can save us all, but I remember how Paul laughed when we first spoke of leaving my tower behind. How he thought it would be a simple thing to leave. He had thought my witch would never suspect. But she did hurt him. I know that Ute has had a plan all along now, something—no, not something, *this.* My life has been preparation for this, even my journey so far that I thought had taken me out of her grasp—but here I am, back doing what she wills. Perhaps if I had told the group sooner of Ute's visits and what I learned . . . But it is too late now. There is no scheme they can wield together without these little ones losing their lives, just as these other children have already been sacrificed for her power. I have to at least try to save these two. I must. Out of the corner of my eye, I see my mother shake her head, but I didn't listen when I should have, and now there is no other way. "I will go with you."

HER POWER

The depth of this mountain castle is astounding to me. We travel deeper and deeper, and I can't imagine how we could have plumbed its depths to find her lair on our own, as our little team was trying to do. What had Paul been thinking? There would be no escape that way. I will have to do this alone. I will have to free myself and the children alone.

I look at the scrawny things; she doesn't even keep them clothed. They must be so weak—no wonder their cries are so pale and pitiful. My heart aches to hold them each in turn, to gather them into my arms and comfort and nourish them.

My witch once asked me how I would ever have a family when I was always running away. Have I just run away again? My mind cannot stop thinking of the look on Paul's face as we moved away, as though I had plunged Ute's knife and lodged it between his ribs, the ribs he said he would have given for the creator to make me.

I must stop thinking of Paul. My mind must concentrate, think of a way out of this. There must be a way to save myself and these little ones.

Somehow . . . my mind is a distracted whirl. I gasp as we begin passing through solid matter as though it isn't there. I cannot think how her magic works as the darkness swallows me. Am I blind?

All at once, we are in her lair and I can see once more. This feels like a dungeon. I shudder and think back on the dungeons I have been in before. My heart quakes, but I remind myself that if I survived my past, surely I can survive this. The sound of dripping has been joined by the sound of water lapping. A burning green light glows nearby. My eyes ache momentarily until I grow used to its brightness. What is it that I am staring at? I can see that she is no longer hovering—she has come to rest, standing on the edge of what looks to be a lake. The iridescent green light spreads its glow to the lake with a sickly cast of yellow.

Ute pushes the children out of her arms and suspends them so they hover in the air. Their weak cries have almost ceased. Her voice moans, and then she is muttering in that deep, earthy language. I don't have to know the language to sense she is calling, calling. Why must I be helpless, no longer empowered to do what must be done? She holds out her hands, and the children slowly levitate away from her to hover over the heart of the lake. I see there is a hole in the ceiling, and pale light glides in from the distant night sky to rest on the children.

Ute motions gracefully with her long hands, her curved fingernails like sharp, pointed knives gesturing for each child to rotate. The waters below begin to swirl as well, while Ute continues to chant. It is deep and eerie, her voice hollowed out by the mystery of the darkness of sin. She cries in a guttural gasp.

I am thrust into the air, pulled into the dance with the children above the waters that are now spinning into a whirlpool. Ute floats to the side of us, keeping us in motion. The gentle lapping sound has now given way to the rushing of waters that spit and spray, recalling to mind the last time I felt at peace. I stood with my beloved looking out over the waves that crashed upon the rocks. The light from that tower—how many ships had it saved from the depths of the sea, from the crash against the rocks that would have destroyed their bulks, opened their bellies, spilling out the lives into the saltwater, crushing lives upon the rocks?

What is it my beloved told me once? That in the darkness, God's light would shine the brightest? I can't see his light here, unless it is the little from the night sky so high, high above us. I can't see his purpose here. These poor children—how many have died before them? They deserve much more, so much love—but people who were supposed to protect them sacrificed them for want of more: more children, more power. They are being used by the sorcery that reaches deep within, calling out the depths of depravity, the need for self-love, for power, for dominance.

As Ute begins chanting the names of her sisters, I feel my chest beginning to ache, throbbing as though my ribs are being slowly pulled apart. My heart is pumping harder, faster; my feet and legs are chilled by the spray from the waters swirling beneath me. She begins chanting the names of the places where her sisters are, the path they must take to find her. I feel as though evil is drawing near, but Jacob said that if I were to call on the name of God's Son, I would find him near. How can I find God near in this place? In the very heart of evil itself? How, oh how? I am alone here, and I cannot save these children, I cannot help them to safety. I was foolish to think I could.

I shriek as my heart is ripped from my chest, and I watch as the same happens to the other two. Ute has now joined us now, and we dance in a circle, her face a mask of hunger. She is crying out, calling into the depths for the Evil One to grant her the power she longs for. I see as her own heart comes forward and all of our hearts nearly touch each other.

"Jesu! Please, save us!" The pain is excruciating. The words are torn from me as the babe and then the toddler whimper and pass out, limply swirling in the air. Have they died? Is it too late? If it hurts this horrifically for me, surely it is too much for them! "Save us, Lord, don't let the Evil One win! I cannot do it." I sob as I recognize my own helplessness, my fallibility. What if I had called on God at the beginning of this journey? What if I had been honest with Paul, and trusted those God had partnered me with? What if I had not allowed fear to—

The light beneath me shoots up, and Ute roars with rage. I feel my heart fly back inside my chest. The sound of women crying claws the air, piercing my eardrums. The water erupts and the cave shakes. Boiling hot, the water shoots up fast and hard, catching me in its wake, pushing me up toward the night sky. The children and I are encompassed in a massive bubble of protective air, and I grab them each to my chest as we shoot up out of the mouth of the mountain. We land in a heap in the snow that is quickly melted and refrozen into a strange pattern of ice crystals all around us.

Ute is flung out near us, but she was not protected by a bubble of air. The water has burned her, and her skin is raw and cratered with blisters. Her cloak is soaked as she screams in pain, and then the air freezes the fabric and water to her skin. She yelps and whimpers, her body shriveling until it becomes a frozen statue.

I pray aloud as it dawns on me that she is dead. "Oh, God, please!" I moan. I tuck the children awkwardly within the bodice of my surcoat to keep their naked bodies warm. I cannot brace us for the avalanche of the ground beneath me as the side of the mountain suddenly gives way. I'm sliding down the jagged rocks on my back, and my hands flail, reaching, grasping—but I keep falling. "Please, God, save us!" I scream again. Hot tears on my face quickly freeze as the rock beneath me shreds my clothes and tears at my skin.

All at once, there is nothing beneath me—and for a moment, I free-fall, then land on a tiny ledge. The babes are squirming, wetting through my clothes. I dare not stand, for the ledge is so narrow. I weep with the little ones. If I relax or move slightly, we will fall off the shelf. Why did God free us only to let us die this way?

Trembles shake me off and on for . . . I don't know how long. The little ones exhaust themselves and pass out as I stare out into the dark night.

After a time, I realize the mountain will not give way further. I almost nod off. With a jerk, I awake, almost falling, but manage to catch myself. In the darkness, a star lights the night sky and grows brighter and brighter still. I have to turn my eyes away as it comes closer to me. In front of me, I see a man who is not merely a man. He is bright and shining, his voice like rushing waters, with a double-edged sword shooting from his mouth and hair white as snow. I know who he is, he is the beginning and the end. He is my Savior and the Savior of these children.

"I am yours, Lord—whatever you will of me, you have it. I will do whatever you say." More hot tears on my cheeks chill instantly.

"I know." His voice is louder than the quaking that erupted the heart of the mountain. "You are mine, and I have called you before the beginning of time. Rest in me, and I will teach you how to serve me."

RECONCILIATION

"Rapunzel! Rapunzel!" I hear Paul's voice calling me from far away as the morning light whispers puffs of golden yellow across the sky. He must be somewhere above my ledge, and I can hear the smile on his face as he says, "If only I could lower my hair to help you up."

I don't know if I'm laughing or crying; maybe it's both.

"I'm tossing you a rope—just hold tight until you get it."

"Hold tight to what?"

"Hope!" I hear Amis shout from somewhere above.

"Or the side of the cliff!" Paul laughs, and I hear a rope skittering over the rocks. The light becomes a bit brighter, and I reach for the shadow that looks like a long snake reaching for me. It is an uncomfortable thing to tie a harness around oneself with two squawking, wet babes inside the bodice of your surcoat, and once I succeed I have no strength left. I have to rely on my friends to pull us up. Bit by bit, jerk by jerk, we begin to ascend. I brace myself to cradle the babes as best I can when we hit against the side of the mountain.

My body is sore, and I'm panting when they finally pull me up and over. Paul pulls me to himself and then jerks backward when the babes protest his hug. "What!?"

"I saved the babes—well, God above saved us." I can't hold myself up anymore. But before I fall to the ground, my mother is there to soften my landing. She retrieves the babes from between my layers of dress and wraps them in our cloaks. "These little ones need attention, and, Rapunzel—" I meet her eyes with my own "—I'm so glad you're safe."

Why can't I stop crying? I look at my mother, tenderly holding the little ones as she walks. Here is a woman who has endured much in her life, both pain and devastation. She is stronger and wiser than I gave her credit for. Gratitude for her overwhelms me.

We have found a trail of some sort, though it doesn't appear to be the one that led us up the mountain. Jacob is preoccupied with helping my mother over the rough path toward a fire Amis has started at the side of the trail.

"How did you find me? What happened when I—when I left you?"

"We spent the night praying for your deliverance until Amis stopped us."

The fool gives a startled laugh. "Well, of course I stopped you! The Lord said to run, and so we had to run."

I stare in awe. "You knew to leave?" I can see that we are quite a ways down the mountain, on a part of the path we traversed days earlier. But how is that possible?

"This fool led us through the castle's cavern and found a new way out. Paul and I will go back in a little while and look for the horses." Jacob pauses, his dark eyes wary. "Should we be watching for Ute?"

"No." My throat threatens to close over the words. "Ute is dead. I—I called out in the name of Jesu, and he delivered us. The mountain spewed us out, but we were cocooned in some sort protective bubble, while she was—she was killed." I take a deep breath and look straight into Paul's troubled eyes. "I should never have gone with her. I was wrong for leaving you." I look over at Jacob. "I just felt I was the only one who could save us."

Paul drops his gaze, but Jacob nods and admits, "I have made mistakes like this before. I thought pulling Paul to the side was the best way to guide him, but I caused dissension, mistrust. We didn't always work together as a team should. That was my fault."

My husband puts his arm around me. "Rapunzel, did you think I was keeping something important from you? I—we weren't. We were trying to figure out how to get the horses safely over the terrain, how to stretch our supplies—and I just don't know yet how to lead. Jacob was trying to teach me how to guide you."

How can my brave husband be so insecure at times? I think of his journey ahead, an entire kingdom to lead one day. I've met his father, the man who never prepared him for this undertaking. The greedy man who was willing to sacrifice his grandson to strengthen his kingdom. Now I feel the fool, but before I begin to cry again, he lifts my chin. "I am sorry to have kept this from you. I didn't mean to make you feel unwanted or unimportant. I didn't realize how things had been twisted until you left with Ute. I thought I lost you."

"I should never have kept Ute's confidence. I should have trusted all of you. It was just—learning the witch had been raising me to become like her shook me. I thought maybe your father was right."

Paul gives a bitter laugh, and shakes his head. "My father is many things, but he is power-hungry and I would never trust his judgment of you. Don't you know how much I love you?"

I can't speak for a moment. This seems too much for me. "Even though—"

Jacob's voice helps me as it breaks through my fears. "Even though they thought to make you like them, God had better plans for you."

Tears fall, but they are cleansing. I take a deep breath. There is one other person I must make amends with. I stare at my mother, who is standing near the fire's warmth while swaying with the little ones. "Mother—"

She lifts her head to look at me, but doesn't stop her swaying. "You needn't apologize to me, Rapunzel. I am forever in your debt for the wrong I did you when you were—"

"No, I forgave you, and I love you. I'm sorry I've been so angry. I could never have made it through this trip without your help, without your wisdom."

"Ha! You say I'm wise?" But the smirk on her face says she is pleased.

It is quiet for a time, and Amis has gathered bits and pieces of foodstuffs from his bag for us to dine on until we find the horses and the rest of the supplies.

"Well, friends," Jacob starts as we begin to eat, "let us thank our God and maker for the mercy he has granted. We have a long way before we reach home, but we are safe now."

"Safe now?" Amis laughs as he sits down on the hard ground. "That reminds me of a story."

WANT MORE NOW?

Can't wait for *Under the Curse* to come out? My gift to you is a free ebook, *Before the Tower*. I hope this taste will make you hungry for more of the journey.

You may be familiar with the original Brothers Grimm story of Rapunzel. But do you know who the witch was before she practiced magic?

Cursed as a young girl, how will Eufemia's longing for power deny her love?

Eufemia and Katterina have normal sister squabbles. They struggle to help their parents put food on the table and look forward to having their own families someday. Katterina discovers *someday* is closer than she thought, but only if she accepts the love of the young man Eufemia might be interested in.

Apprenticed up in a cove in the Soontrisse Mountains to an old widow whose health is failing, Eufemia finds out the woman is not what she seems. Katterina becomes suspicious; what is Eufemia really learning?

Can the sisters learn to navigate their new lives and achieve their desires without harming one another, or is it already too late?

JOIN my newsletter when you download your free copy of *Before the Tower* by visiting https://dl.bookfunnel.com/wftepfzx96. So happy to have you along on the journey!

A QUICK NOTE TO THE READERS

When we began this journey together, Rapunzel was all alone in a wrecked field of sunflowers. Once upon a time I thought the story would be a short story, but then it became a book, and then two, and now her journey has spanned a trilogy. Her story has ensnared others along the way and even as I write this, I am working on the next book after this one. What a joy it has been to write for you. Thank you, from the depths of my soul, for coming along on the journey.

If you have enjoyed this book, please leave a review on whatever retailer you purchased the book through, as well as on GoodReads.

Thank you! It has been the joy of my life to write for you!

Turn the page for a sneak peek at *Under the Curse*!

The words were barely out of Prince Edmund's mouth when Gwynndolen's fist collided with his jaw. He hadn't expected her to hit so hard. In truth, he hadn't expected her to hit him at all.

She struck him again, and he stumbled backward in shock while her brothers snickered. "Shut your mouths!" she commanded, and one by one, they stopped, suddenly more interested in their weapons of choice. "How dare you?" she spat at Edmund, and he wondered if her fury would turn her eyes as red as her hair.

"I meant nothing by it." His breath was visible in the cold spring air, and he tenderly touched his jaw, which ached to the roots of his teeth.

"I never took you for a liar, Your Highness."

"Gwynndolen, you can't say—" her brother Georgius began, but she cut him off.

"I'll speak the truth to whoever needs to hear it! The prince needs to hear it. Rapunzel left you and she's gone, it's true, but that doesn't make her less for not choosing Your Highness. If you were a better man, I would think you would wish her well—especially since she had to escape a witch to find her love."

At this, her brothers chortled but stopped at the flash of her eyes as she turned once more to them. "You men, what do you know of love?" She turned back to the prince, and her look seemed to pierce his very core. "Was she really who you wanted, or were you just making her what you wanted?" She stepped over to her stallion and mounted, leaving Edmund behind in dumb silence.

Only when she was safely out of hearing distance did Georgius laugh aloud, and his brothers joined in. He sheathed his sword and walked over to Edmund, clapping the prince on the shoulder and then roughing his sandy hair with a massive paw. "Don't mind Gwynndolen. She's a bit much at times, but she's also the best horsewoman I know. She'll cool down and still be able to help you later."

The prince wasn't sure how he felt about that. The lady had looked ready to kill him. He had noticed that she and Rapunzel had become close the summer before, but he didn't realize a careless word would cause her to attack him. The brothers seemed to shrug off the incident and surrounded him again with their weapons raised. He returned to practice instead of going for the riding lesson. He parried, thrusted, and dodged till his body was sore enough that he no longer took much notice of his jaw. Not much.

∝≈∝

Rapunzel sat up all at once. "What's wrong?" Paul murmured, peeking open his eyes but only seeing dim outlines of his wife's moving form next to him in the darkness.

"I thought I heard something."

"You didn't hear anything. The baby is fine, go back to sleep."

"I will, but—"

"Rapunzel, she's fine. Let the nursemaid handle things tonight. Let's get one night of sleep—" He reached through the darkness for her, but she was too quick.

"I'll be back in a moment, my love." She slipped from beneath the sheets and padded away toward Helena's room, shutting the door softly behind her.

Paul grunted and stretched. It wouldn't be long . . it was the same game every night. Soon the door creaked open, and the sound of his wife's steps came closer. She pushed the babe towards him, saying, "Hold Helena while I climb in, please."

He didn't argue, but reached out and pulled the baby up close to him. "Why are you awake, little one? You should be sleeping." The babe, who would soon be toddling, giggled at his voice and swiped at him with a moist hand she had obviously been sucking on. "She seems fine to me, Rapunzel."

"Oh, you didn't hear her when I went into her room. She was so sad. The nursemaid had just finished feeding her and, Paul, she needed me."

"She needs to sleep."

"She can sleep with us."

"She needs to sleep in her own room. The nurse can—"

"The nurse doesn't know her like I do. God entrusted her to me! I need to be the one taking care of her."

He sighed, knowing she would have her way in the end, but he frowned into the darkness. It wouldn't be this way forever. Shifting his body, he made room to tuck Rapunzel into his side as she tucked Helena into hers. Paul longed to enjoy this moment, but he couldn't. The babe made chattering sounds, and he ached. He had grown to love holding his wife and the child this way. How hard it would be when he and Rapunzel sent for Helena's family. It was one thing to give his nephew back to his brother— they would see him again. But Helena seemed like their own child after a winter together. Would his wife be able to let go? Would he?

GLOSSARY

Chemise – a slip-like gown that was worn as the first layer of dress for women in Rapunzel's world. It would be naturally colored, typically an off-white color. Often, this was worn as a nightgown when the other layers of dress would be removed.

Cotehardie – a fitted gown worn over the chemise with sleeves cut to various lengths according to station in Rapunzel's world. The higher the station, the more intricate the sleeves, sometimes tight at the elbows and bell-shaped at the wrist or short at the elbows with a streaming tail called a tippet. The bottom of the cotehardie might also be lined with fur to show off the station of a woman.

Coven – in Rapunzel's world, this is a grouping of warlocks and witches that gather in secret to practice the dark arts to return their world back to an acceptance of sorcery.

Handfasting – a wedding ceremony practiced in the Northlands and Alleria at dawn while both the moon and the sun are present in the sky at dawn.

Hosen – leggings worn to protect the legs.

Inner bailey – another term for a castle's inner courtyard within defensive walls.

Sorceress/Sorcerer – a female or male who has achieved a master status in the practice of the dark arts of magic.

Surcoat – the outermost layer of dress a woman would wear in Rapunzel's world, though she would wear a cloak over all in cool weather. The gown was sideless and would complement the cotehardie's coloring, often cut a bit short if the cotehardie beneath had a fur-lined hem. The surcoat was frequently embellished with embroidery.

Wimple – a piece of delicate white linen wrapped beneath the neck and often worn by married women in Rapunzel's time to cover their hair.

YOUR JOURNEY

1. In *Within the Spell*, Rapunzel believes that if she tries hard enough, she will be worthy of her happy ending and her life will be normal. Do you relate to her feelings of inadequacy as the storyline advances? How so?

2. When Katterina shares with Rapunzel more of where she came from, Rapunzel struggles with anger and unforgiveness, even though she had previously committed to forgiving her mother. Have you ever experienced this in your own life? If Rapunzel were a close friend, what would you advise her to do with her feelings?

3. Throughout this first trilogy set, Rapunzel has felt over and over that there was "a Hand guiding her," but she struggles with the idea that anyone else, whether it's God or the witch or Ute, has plans for her. Do you wrestle with such thoughts yourself?

4. When you are feeling as though others are trying to control you, what do you do?

5. In the 29th chapter of Jeremiah, God's beloved people are returning from exile and he promises them that He has great plans for them, "For I know the plans I have for you, declares the LORD, plans for welfare and not for evil, to give you a future and a hope."[1] What plans did the witch and Ute have for Rapunzel? Contrast those with the plans God says He has.

6. Rapunzel realizes at the end of the book just how much she needs God and those He has given her to work together with. Can you brainstorm a healthy way to repair each relationship whose trust has been torn?

7. What types of activities do you think would help heal the weary travelers over the long winter months? What do you think they should do to help one another?

8. Finally, do you think that Rapunzel still wants a normal life? How do you envision her future?

---

1. *ESV*, Jeremiah 29:11.

ALSO BY JACQUELINE VAUGHN ROE

THE JOURNEY SERIES

Before the Tower (*free prequel*)

dl.bookfunnel.com/wftepfzx96

Beyond the Tower

authorjroe.com/book/beyond-the-tower

Amidst the Castles

authorjroe.com/book/amidst-the-castles

Within the Spell

authorjroe.com/book/within-the-spell

Under the Curse

authorjroe.com/book/under-the-curse

Among the Kingdoms (*coming 2021*)

authorjroe.com/book/among-the-kingdoms

NONFICTION AS JACQUELINE V. ROE

Memoirs of a Headcase: Held by the God of Hope

authorjroe.com/book/memoirs-of-a-headcase-held-by-the-god-of-hope

ACKNOWLEDGMENTS

I never feel more inadequate in my writing career than when it is time to say, "Thank you!" but once more, I'll give a try!

Always, I must begin with my Lord and Savior. Without You, my life would be forfeit! I pray my little stories will draw more to You!

Jeff, you are the only man I could live this crazy and hectic life with. I praise God you chose me! Katie, Sydney, and Caleb, you are the most amazing children I could ever hope to have. I can't wait to see where God leads you!

Martha and Russell, thank you for the gift of your son, your love, and your support.

John and Jo, your legacy of love and faithfulness live on. Margaret, thank you for joining us. Joy, I will always miss you. Jeanine and Jessica, how have we survived this past year? With laughter and tears. I love you so much! Allison and Lora, I thank God for you.

Uncle Doug and Aunt Celia, it means everything to live near you at last. Jennifer, you are an astoundingly strong and kind wonder woman. Mike, Heather, Josh,

Travis, and Sean, at last I have written a book with a little more action—and it's all because of you!

Jody, you are an answer to prayer as friend and editor. Without you, my participles would all dangle and I'd never have taken the indie publishing leap. Beth, Rapunzel's journey has continued to astound me as it becomes more physically demanding. I am incredibly blessed by your insight and expertise in movement and love all I'm learning through Fit2B. Allison and Mary, your insight as betas has refined the story and I'm so thankful for you.

Gwynn, though we never got around to starting our JacQuelineandGwynnie University, I'm so thankful that our different paths have not kept us apart. Your prayers have encouraged me throughout the years. Kelly and Rachel, Mom and Dad2, my adoption into the pack was not by chance, God continues to use each of you to mold me to be more like Him. And (always) thank you for the coffee! Lauren, Heather, and Kevin, will we ever stop laughing? NO! And I'm so very, very grateful that you keep me moving towards Jesus. Sara and Mandy, the safe place of hilarious wisdom has strengthened me.

Erica, I continue to be astounded by how God uses you to teach me and others in this chronic life. Mandy, Wendi, and Debbie, your sweet encouragement, prayers, and letters have made all the difference on dark days. I want to hug each of you in person! Karen, Bree, Hollie, Beverly, Tracey, and Erin, I am so thankful for your friendship and prayers. Tiffani, Candice, Linda, and Ruth, thank you for your love and prayers and wisdom.

Finally, to my favorite readers Sara, Eva, Justin, Sophie, Ethan, Emory, Phoebe, Harrison, and Grace. You are each precious to me and I love knowing we are on this journey together!

ABOUT THE AUTHOR

A lover of books and fairytales, JacQueline uses her faith and life experience with chronic pain/depression to discover new ways of telling old stories as well as her own. She lives in North Alabama with her amazing karate husband and three book-crazy children. She takes every opportunity to drink coffee while wearing dangly earrings and the color purple. Join her newsletter when you download your free copy of *Before the Tower* by visiting dl.bookfunnel.com/wftepfzx96.

Find JacQueline at AuthorJRoe.com, and you can also follow her on social media:

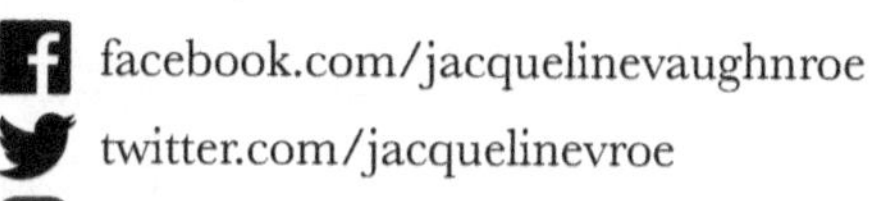